HOLLY EVER AFTER

PASSPORT TO LOVE SERIES

ANNA FOXKIRK

Copyright © 2021 by Anna Foxkirk

All rights reserved.

Second edition published in 2023.

No part of this book may be reproduced in any form or by any electronic or mechanical means, including information storage and retrieval systems, without written permission from the author, except for the use of brief quotations in a book review.

This book is a work of fiction. All characters and events in this publication, other than those clearly in the public domain are fictitious and any resemblance to real persons living or dead, is purely coincidental.

Please note that although Anna Foxkirk is an Australian author, American English has been used in this novel.

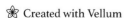 Created with Vellum

Holly Ever After is dedicated to my wonderful mother (née Eileen Foxkirk) with whom I share a birthday, and without whom Christmas would never be quite the same.

ABOUT THE AUTHOR

Voted Favorite Debut Romance Author of 2020 by the Australian Romance Readers Association, Anna Foxkirk writes contemporary romance and historical fiction full of love, laughter and happy ever after...

After gaining an MA in Modern History from St Andrew's University, Scotland and completing training at the Royal Military Academy Sandhurst, Anna served as an officer in the British military for seven years (including four operational military tours in war-torn Bosnia (one with Special Forces) and living in Edinburgh Castle). Nowadays, when she's not writing or reading, she enjoys a quiet(ish!) life working as an English and humanities teacher.

Her love of adventure, romance and humor blaze a trail through her stories.

Anna Foxkirk is an award-winning author. Her first novella, *Alice in Wanderlust*, was published in November 2020 as *Double Trouble* in the *Love and Fireworks* anthology, and in the same year she was voted Favorite Debut Romance Author of 2020 by the Australian Romance Readers Association.

It's Anna's dreams to become a full time writer. If you like what you read, please leave her a short review or email her (annafoxkirk@gmail.com) to let her know

If you'd like to find out more, why not check out her website:
https://www.annafoxkirk.com
And finally, you'll also often find her on Instagram:
https://www.instagram.com/annafoxkirk/

FOREWORD

Thanks for choosing to read *Holly Ever After*. I hope you have as much fun reading this as I had writing it. It gives you a taste of my *Passport to Love* romcom series. The characters are lightly linked, but they're really standalone novellas in the same fish-out-of-water, escapist vein.

If you want to be the first to learn about my other upcoming releases, please sign up to my newsletter. If you think other readers might enjoy this story, then please don't forget to leave a review. It helps them to find me (and, admittedly, will also make my happy ever after!).

Holly Ever After started as a short story some years ago. I think it was lurking in a dark recess of my brain, wanting to see the light of day. Part of it is inspired by my own childhood days at prep school in frostbitten Yorkshire and part comes from my teaching experience both in England (when I had a stationery storeroom at the back of my classroom, but never found myself locked in!) and in Australia.

I'm sorry to say, nothing quite as exciting ever happened in any school stationery closet where I worked, but they have on occasion been a place to escape and dream up stories...

1

Holly

I'm standing at the front of class, it's the last period of the school day, one of the boys in the front is frantically wriggling in his chair and waving his hand and my mind goes completely blank. What on earth did I have planned to teach the kids?

"Yes, Charlie?"

"I thought you said we had carol practice this lesson."

"Oh." I knew I had somewhere I had to be. Five minutes ago. "Blow, you're right! We'd better get a move on."

I herd the children out of the classroom trying and failing miserably to look like a calm and collected adult. "Quick, quick, shift your bums ... but no running!" Running is not permitted in the hallowed corridors of Burtonbridge School.

Waiting in the Great Hall is Stephanie Dawson, my supervising teacher (and nemesis), and the rest of Year Six. Clearly irritated by our late arrival, she taps her watch. "Come along, Six H, we haven't got all day."

"Sorry! My fault," I gasp, trying to catch my breath after our 'speed walking'. "Right, find a spot. That's it, Year Six, no more than ten of you on each step." I chivvy them up the mahogany staircase of the entrance hall.

There are muffled sniggers. "Year *Sucks*, no more than ten of you—"

"Quiet, Sebastian!" I snap, hearing a little monkey in one of the other class groups making fun of my accent. Being a New Zealander in an English school makes me a constant source of entertainment. I try not to take it personally, even when the teachers have a crack, but it can get a little wearing.

However, right now, we're the ones in the wrong and I don't want to delay things further or dampen anyone's festive spirits. I muster up a cheerful smile, and return to my spot at the bottom of the staircase gazing admiringly at the tiered rows of children. A deep sigh escapes me. Standing beneath the enormous brass chandelier, they look like perfect cherubs and it's impossible not to be swept away by the grandeur of the setting. The wooden banister has been festooned with swathes of green foliage and gold tinsel. Behind them, the afternoon winter sun shines in jeweled shafts through the enormous stained-glass window. The oak-paneled walls, the log fire blazing in the enormous stone hearth, the towering Christmas tree tastefully decorated in red and gold all add to the Dickensian atmosphere of the Great Hall. How incredibly English and traditional the whole scene is. How many years, decades even, has Burtonbridge School celebrated Christmas in this manner? It blows my mind just thinking about it.

A small audience gathers alongside us at the bottom of the stairs, including — I can't help noticing out of the corner of my eye — the principal (known here as the headmaster). Chests puff and the volume of singing increases, including my own. We're nearly done and I'm pelting out the carol along with the kids, feeling immensely proud, when Stephanie Dawson raises her hand bringing everything to a screeching halt.

"What on earth are you singing, Tiffany?"

There is snickering in the ranks. Poor little Tiffany on the bottom step looks terrified. She's one of the youngest kids in my class, a shy girl whose eyes have widened to the size of dinner plates at having been singled out. She glances in my direction, and I smile reassuringly.

"Well, Tiffany?" prompts Stephanie.

"Ah...Dick the horse...with...um...bits of holly, Mrs Dawson?" says Tiffany in her breathy voice.

Stephanie Dawson's shoulders stiffen and the kids fall about sniggering. "*Dick* the horse? Lord preserve us! *Deck the halls*, Tiffany, *with boughs of holly*, boughs as in branches, not *bits*! I know you like your ponies, but I can assure you there are no horses with bits of anything in this carol!" She throws me another glare and, head down, the headmaster wisely ducks into his office.

Terrific. Once the laughter has been reined in, we continue. *Tis the season to be jolly, fa-la-la-la-la-la-la-la-la.*

I sing on, somewhat subdued and avoiding everyone's eyes. Tiffany's cheeks are glowing redder than Rudolf's nose, and I get the feeling she'd quite like to disappear up the chimney. She's not the only one.

Once our rehearsal is over, the children disperse, and I shuffle back to the quiet of my classroom feeling a bit on the gloomy side of festive.

Outside, the sky is now dark. For a while, I sit with my head in my hands listening to the sound of students leaving: a rabble on the march, shouting, singing – *Dick the horse* – and being driven away in their parents' Jaguars and Range Rovers.

It doesn't seem so very long ago since I was part of that mad scramble to get away from school, though my state school in Auckland couldn't have been more different to this place. Set in more than one hundred acres on the edge of the North Yorkshire moors, Burtonbridge School was founded over three hundred years ago. I suspect some of the staff might be almost as ancient. It still feels like a fluke I got my teaching degree (I'm the first uni student in my family) let alone this teaching position in the UK. It should feel like a dream come true, but most days, I feel like I'm just one of the kids who's dressed up to look the part — the biggest prankster in school. The same prankster who used to hurl paper darts, or pull smart-ass faces whenever the teacher's back was turned. Perhaps it's my imposter syndrome, but I keep expecting the headmaster to stride into my classroom at any moment, bushy eyebrows bristling, and announce, *Sorry, Hadaway, did we say you were awesome? We meant awful. Truly awful! You're trash. Trailer trash. You don't even know how to speak English properly. Your vowels are mangled and your background...well, let's not even go there.*

Taking a breath, I drag my eyes back to the computer screen and open up the school reports I've still not finished. Only one more week. One more week and I'll have made it through my first term of teaching in England and it'll be the holidays. Then and only then I can collapse. For now, the promise of Christmas and the season to be jolly hangs out of reach, like the golden star on top of the Christmas tree.

"Still here, Holly?" says Stephanie Dawson, poking her head around the classroom door and scaring the hell out of me.

"*Jeepers!* I–I–yes. I thought everyone had left." I put a hand over my heart. It's going like the clappers. "Just giving my reports a final once-over, then I'll go home."

"Oh. Those should have been submitted already," she says, frowning, "but at least you're being conscientious, I suppose. I can't tell you how tired I am of correcting errors in other teachers' reports. I'd rather you didn't add to my list of work."

"I won't add to your list—"

"*List*, Holly, not *lust*. Dear God!" She flicks her hair. "Email them straight through to me as soon as you've finished. I might get a chance to look at them tonight."

"Okay."

"Right then. Goodnight. You definitely know what you're doing?"

Does she mean teaching in general, or simply how to submit my reports via the archaic and totally non-intuitive IT school management system?

"Actually—"

"Good. I'd stay and help, but I still haven't got my outfit sorted for the staff Christmas party." She twiddles her fingers at me. "Toodleoo!"

Closing the door, she disappears before I have a chance to ask for her help. Sounding like a well-shod horse, she clip-clops along the wooden floorboards of the corridor. There's the faint swish of the double doors, and then I'm all alone with my thoughts again.

Toodleoo my left foot! Who even says stuff like that these days? Maybe I should insert it into a report somewhere. Little Harry has made toodleoo progress this term! Dear Jemima's toodleloo precociousness is toodleoo unbelievable. I delete yet another homophone error — *there* instead of *their* — thanking my lucky stars I spotted it before I send my reports in. Writing school reports is like navigating a minefield, one wrong word and — *poof!* — it could be my last Christmas party ever. *Bloody fancy-dress Christmas party!* I'd rather not go, but I get the distinct impression that would not be the 'done thing' at all.

I hate fancy dress with a passion. I can already envisage me enduring one awkward conversation after another, my work colleagues and their spouses looking baffled or uninterested in any and everything I have to say. It'd be a whole lot easier if I had someone to go with.

Try as I might to focus on my reports, my mind keeps straying to the staff party. It's bad enough having to dress appropriately for school in the daytime, or dressing for a school function in the evening, but fancy-dress is my worst nightmare of all: how am I going to find an outfit that says *fun,* but also *responsible, stylish and definitely not frazzled-Kiwi*?

I stab at the keyboard, trying to delete a formatting error.

Damn!

What the actual...? "Noooo!" The entire document has become a narrow strip of words running down the middle of the screen. Frantically, I hit *Undo, Undo, Undo*...and breathe a sigh of relief when the screen returns to some semblance of normal. That was a sickeningly close call.

Gently, I press at a few more keys.

So, what the heck do I go to this Christmas party as anyhow? Sexy

Santa? Foxy elf? Without thinking I jab the *return* key. Suddenly the screen on my computer shows a blizzard of snow. I throw up my hands. "Noooo! Not again! This can't be happening to me!" It might be Christmas, but this snow can go to hell.

What the actual...?

I swear colorfully, glaring at the computer screen, praying to God, and Santa and all his elves that I have not just lost my precious school reports. A whimper escapes me. I need to reboot myself and this bloody computer.

In a panic, I turn the computer off at the wall and start counting to ten. "One Mississippi...two Mississippi...It's no use trying to count, the blizzard has somehow transferred itself to my brain and I can't even remember how to count.

Yes, you can, Holly! Calm down! Deep breaths!

But fear, unaccountable fear, and frustration and pent up fury rise like an unstoppable tide in my chest. I can hear my breath coming in great heaving gasps. This is not keeping my head above water. I am definitely sinking into a pit of despair...

At moments like this there's only one thing for it — I rush into the stationery storeroom at the back of my classroom and, with my fist in my mouth, I scream. Strange though it may seem, this is my own improvised, but usually effective, cheap-as-chips emotional therapy. It is a good stress reliever. I let off yet another silent scream. I kick the beanbag on the floor. How late am I going to be here at school tonight? I can't leave until the reports are all finished and sent to bloody Dawson. *Breathe, Holly. The computer will probably be working fine again once you switch it back on. You can do this. You've got this. Just breathe. Breathe in, breathe out...*

I throw myself down on the heap of large beanbags I have stashed up against the far wall under the window. A couple more minutes and I'll return to the real world again and face my report writing.

After a minute or two of biting my fist, I manage to get my breathing back under control.

Storeroom is a bit too grandiose a word for this walk-in cubby. In terms of size, I imagine it's not dissimilar to a monk's cell, but with functional wooden shelving lining one side and a tiny arched window, high up on the far wall, that shows a notch of sky and, if I stand on tiptoes, the rooftops of Burtonbridge in the valley below. This cell is where I keep the chaos, and I'm not talking about the classroom supplies – the pens, pencils, files and textbooks – though there's plenty of those. I'm talking about all my emotional baggage, the suppressed angst, homesickness, imposter syndrome, wretched loneliness...I could go on. I sometimes wonder if the teacher I replaced, Phoebe someone-or-other, ever used this room for similar purposes. Perhaps when she was told her husband had been in a terrible accident she came in here...

I'm not usually this negative.

Digging my fingers into the beanbags, I focus on my breathing and the positive experiences I've also had in here. This is where I come when I'm in danger of cracking up laughing because of something hilarious one of the kids has said or done. I also love the reams of paper and all the stationery – I'm a bit of a stationery addict. There's nothing quite like the woody smell of paper—

"Oh for the love of...*Bloody toodleoo!*" I spot the pile of sheets of A3 colored paper I've not yet prepared for tomorrow morning's first activity. How could I have forgotten? Leaping to my feet, I grab a pair of scissors and a wad of the colored paper and return to my beanbag. I start snipping furiously.

First lesson tomorrow, I'm supposed to be decorating the class, making it look thoroughly Christmassy for the children. The students will be making paper chains. But no ordinary paper chains, oh no. My class are going to write nice, positive messages to one another on the paper strips, then link and hang them around the classroom as decorations.

We are only as strong as our weakest link, I'll suggest – or something equally profound.

If we master that, we may progress on to toodleoo paper angels.

2

Clyde

Outside, I hear the muffled sound of church bells. Five o'clock.

Brian, the boss, jumps up from his desk in the corner of the room. "Oh bollocks, I forgot. We still haven't fixed that lock on Miss Hadaway's stationery cupboard door and she cornered me this morning."

"I wouldn't mind being cornered by her!" chips in one of the others.

Brian slips on his coat. "Any chance you could take a look at it, Clyde? Should be a very quick job. Just the lock on the door of her storeroom. I'd do it myself, but I've promised the old lady and kids we'd get our Christmas tree tonight." He looks at me with his hang-dog, bloodhound, eyes.

The man needs more rest and more sleep. Being a father of five kids cannot be easy.

"Aye. No bother. I'll fix it on my rounds, before I lock up," I say.

"Cheers. You're a legend."

Yes, a legendary glutton for punishment, but he's been good

taking me on without the experience most of the other groundsmen have, and like he said, it should be any easy fix. Besides I don't really mind working late. I like hearing the kids running about, but I also like the peace and quiet. There's something calming about early mornings and the end of the day, when the buildings are dead quiet and it's only me and the heating humming around the old place. The empty hallways echo with my footsteps and you can almost hear the laughter of former pupils in the silence. Words and ideas seem to tumble and freefall in the empty rooms with no-one to disturb them but me.

I check the logbook: sure enough, Miss Hadaway has emailed Brian four times about the broken lock on her door. It's not like him not to attend to things more punctually, but perhaps he's pissed off she's been pestering him, or it could be just because we've been that busy, what with putting up all the Christmas decorations and preparing for the Christmas party tomorrow.

Grabbing my toolkit, I set off at a leisurely pace. I check all the classrooms are empty, turning out the lights as I go, locking the doors, shutters and windows, until I get to Miss Hadaway's classroom. For some reason, the hairs on the back of my neck stand on end. I put my toolkit on the floor. She may be new in the school, but Holly Hadaway has already gained a reputation, not for being a typical laid-back Kiwi, but more for being something of a tornado, leaving a trail of destruction in her wake.

Thankfully, she's nowhere to be seen, although, of course, she's forgotten to turn her classroom lights off — pretty typical of most of the teachers in this school.

The likelihood of her being here after six pm is almost nil, I tell myself.

Not almost nil enough as it turns out.

I open the storeroom door to find Miss Hadaway sprawled on a pile of beanbags at the far end. Open-mouthed, she looks as if I've caught her in the middle of doing something inappropriate. Her shocked face is framed by a riot of golden curls and she's pointing a pair of scissors at me as if she's not afraid to use them. For a second, maybe two, I'm stumped, my brain bogged down, unable to form a single intelligent syllable. All sorts of unsettling thoughts enter my head.

Mumbling a half-baked apology and a mangled explanation, I turn my back on her and focus hard on the lock furniture...and not the fact that as she'd scrambled to her feet I caught a glimpse of pink triangle between her legs — *knickers not flesh,* I berate myself.

3

Holly

I thought it was just the old building creaking with the wind, but my paper cutting comes to a severed halt as the door opens and one of the janitors-come-groundsmen-come-general-school-workmen steps in. He's tall and lean and sporting green coveralls. He mumbles something incoherent and I'm momentarily distracted, wondering if I could jazz up his coveralls to turn them into some sort of elf outfit for the Christmas party. Now there's a thought.

"Hi," I say, "I wasn't expecting company."

I scramble to my feet thinking I'll take everything out into the classroom, but he turns his back on me and blocks my path. "I'll get out of your way, shall I? I can do this in the classroom. I was just preparing for Golden Time tomorrow morning."

He mumbles again, something about the broken lock on the door and proceeds to fiddle. Another friendly Brit. Is it because I'm a New Zealander, or because he's embarrassed that it's taken so long for one of the maintenance crew to respond to my emails? If the stationery in this room goes missing, Stephanie has hinted (none too subtly) I'll be blamed (and billed).

There's a noisy exhalation of breath and a muttered expletive from the man. I don't think I'll be asking to borrow his coveralls any time soon.

Standing behind him, my arms weighed down with stationery, I wait for him to step aside, but he doesn't even acknowledge my presence. I might as well be a tube of glue.

"Excuse me." I cough.

Nope, nothing in response.

After a few tense seconds, wondering whether or not I should tap him on the shoulder — impossible considering how much stuff I'm carrying — he says, "Aye, it's stuffed!"

Bravo. Full marks. I think he may be Scottish. "I know it's *stuffed*. I wouldn't have emailed so many times and written it into the school logbook *repeatedly*, if it wasn't stuffed." I start wrestling the sheaves of paper back onto the shelves, feeling suddenly, inexplicably claustrophobic. I need to get out of here immediately. "Whatever you do don't—"

Looking over my shoulder, I see he's closing the door.

"— close the bloody door!"

Too late.

The idiot's closed the door. He wiggles the door handle. "Ach, shite! She's jammed," he says, addressing the door.

For a moment I'm not sure what to say. I stop breathing. The fool had *closed* the door. *Closed us in. The door is buggered and so am I. What about my reports? What about these paper chains. I'm going to be here past midnight!*

Behind his back, I do yet another short silent scream. My brain stalls. And takes its time to kickstart again. Right now, my 'safe' room is feeling less safe by the second. What sort of moron is he, closing the door when he knows there's a problem with the lock?

"Beaut!" I say, with unveiled sarcasm. "Tell me you can fix it quickly."

He says nothing. I stare at the broad bank of his shoulders and my stomach twists into a tight knot.

"I *have* to get out. You *need* to let me past."

He yanks on the metal knob and swears under his breath. "Aye, I'd like to, but ye see it's stuck."

I shoulder him aside. "Yeah...nah, it can't be stuck. Not really."

"Yeah...nah, it totally is."

He's dropped his Scottish burr to mimic my Kiwi accent — hilarious. I don't need the likes of him making fun of me.

Eyeballing one another, we try to outstare each other. But something in his eyes turns my knees to jelly, and I refocus on jiggling the lock.

Nothing doing. "Okay, it's munted."

"Munted? That's a new one on me."

I try not to think about him standing so close. All I can hear is heavy breathing — his, mine, I really don't much care whose — I'm beginning to feel more flustered by the second and very hot beneath my Peter Pan collar. *God help me!* I don't say this out loud of course. I may be working in a Christian school, but I'm not religious, not even remotely, however right now, stuck in the teensy-tiny stationery room with the janitor-come-gardener-come-general-DIY-dogsbody (General Dickhead comes to mind!), even I might get down on my knees and pray.

What is the correct etiquette when you're stuck in a cupboard with a total stranger who has the IQ of a pencil? Okay, perhaps not total stranger: I've seen the dude around school, but that hardly makes him someone I'd want to pass more than two polite seconds with.

"Munted. What does that mean exactly?" he asks.

Any remnants of *polite* make their escape, under the door.

"It means we're screwed! Why did you close the door you idiot? I said not to. I clearly stated in my email the lock on the door is faulty and gets stuck, and now you've gone and got us both trapped in here..." My voice, on the rise like a steaming kettle, reaches a quavering squeal. "Sort it out! That's your job! I need to go home right now! I can't be stuck in here with *you*...I have a date!" A snort of fear escapes me. I have no idea why I lie. The only date I have is with some paper and school reports, but he doesn't need to know that. He doesn't need to know anything about me *at all*, but he *does* need to show a greater sense of urgency than his current comatose state. His eyes are expressive though, I'll give you that. To say I feel diminutive when he slaps me again with his skinned-blue gaze is an understatement. He has the sort of eyes that have spent far too much time in the great outdoors, squinting beneath the glare of the Scottish sun. The sort of eyes that do not like being holed up in dark cubbies with irascible teachers. Piercing knock-you-off-your-Kiwi-feet blue eyes. And now I've been stuck in here trying to avoid them, in stifling proximity — I make a point of checking my watch, giving it a tap (so clearly I've learnt something from Stephanie Dawson) — for approximately five minutes.

4

Clyde

Oh, bollocks! Of all the freakish accidents! This is my bad. My bad bloody disaster!

When Miss Hadaway started trying to make conversation, my brain slowed to sloth speed, my fingers became thumbs and my big foot stumbled against the door, accidentally kicking it closed. And I haven't the heart to admit my tool kit is on the other side of the door. *Shite!*

The main reason I've taken this job was because I thought it would be easy manual work, meaning I'd have plenty of brainpower left in the well to spare for creative thinking. Right now, nothing creative nor even logical about my brain seems to be functioning. I know this is my fault, but I can't sort anything with Hellfire Hadaway breathing down my neck.

It's only as she tells me *she* has a date that I recall I have one as well. I'm meant to be meeting my parents in the White Swan Hotel, or the Mucky Duck as it's more commonly referred to in these parts, in town for dinner at eight. *Double shite!* I'd sworn blind I wouldn't forget or even be late. I wasn't exactly raring to go. It would be fine if it was just me and my folks, but my mother has booked for Olivia to join us too — all part of their ill-disguised scheme to get us back together again. The happy couple. As far as I'm concerned, it isn't happening — not before a monster is spotted doing laps of Loch Ness. I'd rather spend the night in jail.

Funny that, considering my present predicament.

I open my mouth to apologize, but clam it shut again. Looking down at Miss Hadaway, I can't help agreeing with the other lads' gossip. She's hot all right, but in a scud-guided missile kind of way. Tricky to handle and more than likely to blow up in my face.

Up close, Hadaway is fifty shades of pastel, but her Kiwi mouth is running at sixty shades of red, and I'm barely taking in a word. She has extremely kissable lips that she's painted a very festive scarlet. I don't want to be cooped up in here with her a second longer than I need to be, but I can't help feeling awestruck.

Fury emanates from her in waves, and I soak it up like a sponge.

Although, she obviously thinks I'm a complete loofah.

5

Holly

I have a bit of rant; he says nothing. So, finally, I give up.

It's funny how details can hit you in the face when you're least expecting it: when you're snared like a trapped animal. I probably have steam whistling out of my ears, but right now, of all the inappropriate moments, I can't help noticing how unbelievably arresting this janitor dude is — in a totally understated way. Okay, his nose is a bit crooked and his expression guarded...but I swear those eyes could bore holes through metal. He's not unlike one of those rare actors who you don't realize are mouth-wateringly handsome until they become the unsuspecting hero of the day, and by the time you realize your mistake you've fallen irretrievably in lust with them and it's too late to pick yourself up again. Not that I'm in lust. He's not my hero; he's got me stuck in this hole.

I press my face up against the small square of glass in the door. "What a tool!" I say. The comment isn't aimed solely at *him;* I've spotted my mobile phone sitting on the corner of my desk, on the wrong side of the door. So close and yet so far.

Behind me, janitor-man swears under his breath.

I round on him. "Look, I wasn't talking to you. *I'm* the tool. I've left my phone on my desk. You'd better ring someone on yours to get us out of here." I'm not about to give him a full-blown apology mind, not when he's caused the problem in the first place, but hands on my hips, I do my best to smile.

There's a moment as he considers. Cogs grinding slowly. Bit of rust in there slowing things down. He folds his arms and considers me.

"Please," I say. Perhaps a little too late.

"Och…no!"

"Och, no?" I too can imitate accents. I ball my fists at my sides.

Everything about him is too bloody quiet. Un-agitated. Self-contained. Stiller than concrete. It reminds me of some movie I once watched on television about stalking deer, the man waiting for hours before pulling his trigger. His stillness makes me want to jump up and down like one of my students, holler for help, or throw a tantrum.

"Not possible," he says, putting his hands in his pockets.

At that point, I throw him a chilling look; the one that instils quiet and self-preservation in my students. "Why not? I suppose you're going to tell me you're the one person in this day and age who doesn't carry a mobile phone, eh?" My tone is now openly scathing, but he's daring to look unscathed, protected by a force-field of ignorance, or is it arrogance? Whatever! He's getting under my skin like a bloody splinter.

He stares at the ceiling. Compressing his lips, he shakes his head. "Och, man-oh-man. How'm I goin' to live this one down? Imagine the crack when the boys find out I've got myself stuck in the stationery cupboard. With you. I'll never hear the end of it. My reputation is going to be slammed."

"Your reputation! *Your* reputation! What about *my* reputation, you f-fu…muppet! If you don't get us out of here in the next ten minutes, I'm going to make sure you have no reputation to speak of and everyone knows you're not fit for the job!"

There is a very pregnant — I'd say about 39 weeks — pause.

"Tin minutes?"

Mouth-twitching son-of-a-b— "Ten! Ten!" I shout, contorting my syllables, stamping my foot and squeezing my eyes closed.

6

Clyde

So, hang me! I know I'm being a bit of a dick and I shouldn't take the Mickey, but she's like a mini firecracker just begging to be set off. And she's been bloody rude, calling me a *muppet* when she's the one ranting like Miss Piggy. I clamp my lips closed, she stamps her foot, and words just slip out. "I imagine cutting paper and the like must be terribly difficult..."

Her face becomes a work of art.

Cheeks flaming, mouth popping open.

"Oh!" Lips close again. *"You!"* And open.

Chrrrrist alive! I could write a poem about that perfect 'O'.

Oh me, oh my.

To be honest, I'm no longer thinking straight at all; I'm barely functioning as a human, let alone a supposedly creative one. It's as if this woman is transmitting some debilitating disease. I can feel myself transforming, into my father. Monosyllabic. Arms folded.

"Damn!" she says. "No actually, Fuck! Fuckety, fuck, fuck!"

"I barely know you," I say, "but I wouldn't dismiss the idea out of hand...especially as we may be here for some time."

"Oh, shut up! This cannot be happening!" She turns away and her shoulders slump.

I give myself a shake. Maybe I've pushed Miss Hadaway a bit too hard. Now I feel bad. I try to put myself in her shoes — not easy considering they're a pair of delicate pink stiletto heels — trapped alone in here with a clodhopper like me. I reboot my brain and take my phone from my pocket. "Hey, sorry. Look. I do have a phone but it's dead."

When she reluctantly turns back to me, I show her the blank screen and focus extremely hard at maintaining a blank expression to match. "I would call for help, but my battery died a while ago. This phone is a bit of dinosaur."

She huffs and shoves past me. Walks to the door and kicks it. It's probably me she'd like to be kicking. She hammers with her fist to be let out.

I take a seat on her beanbags.

Glaring over her shoulder at me, she has another go jiggling the lock, at first with patience, then with increasing frustration. "Oh, for... for...fudge! This is ridiculous!" Hands splayed against the door, I think she means to rest her head against it, but she more or less headbutts it. Maybe she's not quite so delicate as she first appears. Or a lot more frustrated.

"Headbutting the door is not likely to help, ye ken."

"Well if I was unconscious perhaps this situation would be little more bearable." The words rattle out of her.

My conscience needles me. Strictly speaking, I know this whole situation is my fault, but I can't bring myself to admit it. At this point, I consider it a wise precaution to wait until she's calmed down a bit. Or, I think, perhaps I'm turning into my father who's never admitted anything was his fault in his entire life, not unless it's earning him barrowloads of money. Whatever the case, I need time to consider how to fix the situation and her visible agitation is not helping. She's distracting. Also, admittedly, hot. But also ever-so-slightly unhinged. Honestly though, it's probably a reflection of what the kids put these teachers through these days, particularly at this school. Talk about entitled.

Try as I might, I can't help but notice the back of her stockinged heels, her delicate ankles, her smooth caramel calves that tighten as she bobs up on her toes, the hem of her floaty floral skirt — totally inappropriate for a British winter — wafting about around her knees, perfectly hugging the rounded curve of her backside. I could write an ode to her butt.

Butt that I...

She glares over her shoulder and I quickly look away.

Closing my eyes, I listen to her hammering.

The school is obstinately silent. Like a sulking recalcitrant pupil. Miss Hadaway doesn't give up easily, I grant her that. After about half an hour of persistent knocking and calling out, she finally gives up.

"What are you doing?" she demands.

I open my eyes guiltily. "Nothing."

"Precisely! That's the problem!"

I have a long list of problems, but funnily enough, doing 'nothing' is not on my list. "What would you like me to do?" I ask, noticing her heels are now strewn on the floor. A tripping hazard. I nudge them aside with my foot.

"Leave my shoes alone! Don't touch them!"

I freeze. *Woah!* Her anger seems to have risen a few decibels in the last half an hour. I'd better not touch anything to do with Miss Hadaway in case I cause her to sky-rocket. Though, perhaps I could write an ode to her shoes.

What slender instep have you kissed...

Sometimes I wish my brain would shut up. It's kind of tiring and even I can recognize a cheesy line when I spout one. However, a major problem I'm becoming increasingly aware of is that if I have to spend too much time in here, not touching, not skimming that hem upwards, I might lose my mind. For all my delicate and admittedly not-so-delicate thoughts, I'm a full-blooded male and value my sanity. I need something to do. Thankfully, just when I think I'm close to losing it, I have a flash of inspiration.

"What did you say all these strips of paper were for? Perhaps I could help. I'm quite handy with my hands…" I trail off, ready for her to bite my head off, realizing I've committed yet another faux pas.

From the ways her eyes scout the shelves, she looks like she might be searching for something to throw at me. Stapler. Pens. Scissors.

With a sigh like a Greek heroine, and a thump that makes even the beanbag exhale air, she sits down beside me. Half-heartedly, listlessly, she begins to explain the purpose of the paper strips.

"I was going to ask the kids to make paper chains for Christmas decorations," she says. "The idea was that they write nice positive festive messages on them to try to get us in the Christmas mood…I was going to make a couple of examples to model the idea…only, for some unfathomable reason, I'm really not feeling festive any more." She sighs again.

"Och, I remember making paper chains in school when I was a wee lad. It's a great idea. I ken help you. I'm not so bad with words."

"Sure." She doesn't sound convinced.

I turn toward her, but unfortunately, the scent of jasmine assaults my senses and those pink lips are a bit too bloody close for my sanity. Body parts begin to squeeze. Extracting myself from the beanbag, I stand up. I figure I need to keep a measured distance between us, like about five meters, which is something of a challenge given the tight space we're in.

Don't! Don't even think of tight spaces! Best to think about heating and electricity and plumbing. No, not plumbing either…

7

Holly

"Och, I'm not so bad with words," he says, when I expand on my idea for the kids to write messages on the paper chains. I bet he does. Heaps of one-syllable Scottish words like, *och* and *ach* and *nae* and *ken*. Super useful.

Nevertheless, despite my lack of encouragement, he starts cutting. Picking up another sheet of paper, I join him. Anything to pass the time.

Much to my surprise, like a seedling, our stilted conversation takes on a life of its own and blossoms. He asks me about New Zealand. I give him the tourist synopsis. He tells me a bit about Scotland. He's from the Highlands, somewhere near Inverness. His soft Scottish lilt seems to mellow as he talks and it's actually rather soothing to listen to.

On his feet, I watch him from the corner of my eye, leant up against the shelves, cutting strips of paper with his very clean hands — so clean, I suspect he's not the most diligent or energetic of groundsmen. But they move with confidence. And they look strong. And capable. Clyde Hunter (we've introduced ourselves fully by now but foregone the handshakes) has very capable-looking hands.

I focus on the paper strips. I've always had a bit of a thing about hands, but now is not the time to develop even a morsel of admiration for this man. This situation is his fault, I remind myself.

Our conversation deviates to reading and books. I'm surprised to find out he reads a lot. In fact, I soon realize he's far better read than me, which shuts me up for a bit. First impressions can be very misleading. So can second impressions. But sitting there, I can't help but wonder how on earth Clyde ended up becoming a groundsman when he could be so much more.

So much more of what? Not everyone has your burning ambition, I tell myself. *He's probably perfectly happy with his life...before he was stuck in a cupboard.* He's remarkably sanguine about the whole situation though. Unlike me.

It's hypnotic watching him cut and listening to his dulcet tones. Maybe I'll go and visit Scotland one day. See if all Scots are like him.

Now and again, I flap my hands in mad panic to turn the motion-sensor lights back on.

Once in a while, I stand up, go to the door, and peer wistfully out at my classroom, at my phone sitting on my desk, hoping someone might at some point in the not too distant future notice the lights have been left on and come to free us. I look at my watch. It's gone eight.

"Sorry, about your date," Clyde says.

"What?" *What date? Oh yes, the date I invented.* "Oh yeah, well, can't be helped. I'll explain to him...tomorrow."

"Tell me about him. Your boyfriend." He looks at me with his sharp as tin-opener eyes, and I wonder if he's guessed the truth.

Bugger, why did I lie about having a date? Shrugging I sit down and hunch further over the paper letting my hair hide my face. "Oh, you know...ey?" I concentrate, as if this particular strip is proving particularly challenging.

"Does he have a name, your man?"

"He's not *my* man! People don't own one another!" I snap,

snorting with embarrassment, maybe a bit too emphatic. "It was just a date ... and, of course, he has a name." For no good reason, for some *insane* reason, our illustrious Head of PE pops into my head. Leo Tarrant.

"Leo," I say, leaning back against the wall, cringing at the thought. Leo Tarrant, more crudely labelled at school as Torpedo Tarrant, is quite the specimen of male perfection and makes no bones about coming from 'good stock'...but whatever bones went into that particular stock, they forgot to give him a jaw bone. I couldn't imagine anything worse than a date with Tarrant. His bronzed thighs may be a tribute to manhood, his bulging biceps a gift from the gods...but all no doubt with the help of a slipped steroid every once in a while.

"Och, not the Torpedo!" says Clyde, as if reading my thoughts. He looks appalled. Would Leo Tarrant really be so out of my league?

I find myself bristling. "Is that so unimaginable?"

The cupboard is silent, the clanking rumble of pipes in the building faintly audible.

It takes Clyde a moment to respond. "No, not at all. He's fine. He's a ...a...pal. I simply thought you wouldna' be his..." He trails off again.

I wouldn't be to his type. I bet that's what he was going to say, or something like that. But how would *he* know what Leo's *type* is! I've never seen them hanging out together. They couldn't be more different. Leo probably bought Clyde a beer once upon a time in the pub because he was feeling charitable. I can pretty much imagine Leo's response to the suggestion they might be pals — the curled upper lip.

Clyde settles himself back down beside me, with a smile on his lips. I'm not going to demean myself by worrying about what he is thinking. He can think what he wants of me. Is it really so unlikely that Leo and I would have a date? If he asked me out, I'd say no. But I'm not going to give Clyde the satisfaction of knowing that. He's clearly amused by the whole idea and for some reason that grates.

In silence, we cut until we run out of paper.

Quarter of an hour later when I realize Clyde has stopped cutting, I risk a sideways glance. His head is back, lolling against the wall, and he's staring at the ceiling again. Maybe it's the lighting he finds so fascinating. I can't help noticing his thighs are long and lean. I can't stop myself from wondering what is going on inside that thick skull of his. Who should *he* be with now? To my surprise, I find myself thinking his green coveralls provide the perfect camouflage for his good looks. How did I not spot that profile before? The hard jawline, the dusting of stubble, the soft bump of his mouth—

Oh, bloody hell! Good looks? How long have we been stuck in here – an hour? Two? I'm losing all perspective. My mouth feels parched. I lick my lips.

"So, what were you meant to be doing tonight?" I ask.

8

Clyde

"Nothing much," I say, thinking of my mother, Marjorie's, tears of exasperation and my father, Hamish's, eye-popping fury, "just seeing my parents." To distract myself, I pick up a pen and begin to write on one of the scraps of paper. *Bloody bollocking bawbags*! Dad's going to skin me alive.

"What are you doing with that pen?" asks Holly. It sounds like *pin*. I love her Kiwi accent and can't help but smile. "Don't waste them. I need those paper strips for tomorrow."

"Seriously? You have enough paper strips cut to supply the entire school with paper-chain-making kits."

She twists her mouth back and forth, until a reluctant smile appears and the dimples in her cheeks wink. Damn it, she's too bloody cute. Perhaps it has something to do with her saving me from a fate worse than death, but my heart trips like a faulty sprocket. I continue writing, telling myself it's nothing, it's simply the thought of the humdinger of an argument I'm going to have to face later with my folks. If I ever get out of here. I console myself with the thought that if

I happen to have heart failure now, I'll be fine. All the teachers in school are trained in CPR. *Mouth to mouth resuscitation would be...*

I choke on the thought and disguise it as a cough. "I thought maybe we could give the kids some examples to help them get started. You said you were going to write on a couple of them."

"Oh, yes." She snatches the slip of paper from my hands.

On one side I have written, *Say something nice to the person sitting next to you.*

Her eyes light up and she nods approvingly. "Well done. Good idea," she says. "The *children* need to be positive, show their support for one another, or maybe," she flips over the paper, "they could write N-new Year's reso-res—" She splutters and bites her lip.

On that side of the paper, I've written, *Your lips make me purr.*

She pouts and her lips wiggle again, as if she is no longer certain what to do with her mouth. "Yeah...nah, look, not quite like that. That's a bit left field." Taking a deep breath, she shakes her head and looks me in the eye. Confusion personified. Her mouth a bud. It triggers a very physical reaction in me: the hairs on my arms and the back of my neck rising. My heart silently purring. *Och, down boy.*

She loops and glues the link of paper closed, so only the *Say something nice* side is visible.

"The words need to be appropriate," she says, in her best schoolmarmish British accent. She picks up another of my handwritten strips and reads aloud. "Write a compliment about someone you don't often speak to." She laughs. "That'll be us then." She flips it over again. "Rap me in paper. What does that mean? How is that even a compliment? You're missing the point. And if you're talking about wrapping, like for Chrissy pressies, *wrap* is spelt with a 'w'." She slaps the paper down on the floor between us.

I pick it back up. "Och, but that depends on what sort of rap you're talking about. I had rhythm and poetry in mind. That sort of RAP. You know, it's an abbreviation."

She gives me a look. I wonder if I'm too large to crawl under the bottom shelf.

"Not even…Of course." She repositions herself so she's sitting more upright. Leaning as far away from me as is physically possible.

9

Holly

The cupboard is cold, but my cheeks feel like they could fry an egg. I can't help but imagine the rhythm and poetry Clyde might have in mind the way he looks at me. The noise we would make on these beanbags. *Never*! He's not my type.

He stands up, stretching. Like a caged animal, he paces a couple of steps toward the door, turns, and paces back in my direction. Back and forth he goes, several times, until cracking his knuckles, he sits back down again.

At that point, I jump to my feet. It's childish. But he makes me jittery. I take my time tidying the pieces of paper away, placing strips neatly back into boxes on the shelves, tucking his paper strips at the very bottom, as if hiding incriminating evidence. At the same time as trying not to show I am interested in what he's written, heart hammering, I read snatches — *helping hand* mingles with — *plumb your depths —*

"*Strewth!*" I disguise my reaction as a sneeze. Goosebumps pepper my skin and I rub my hands up and down my arms. Is it normal to go from hot to cold in a flash like this? "What's wrong with the heating in here?" I snap. "We're going to die of hypothermia before anyone finds us."

He lumbers to his feet and we sidestep around each other.

As if we're dance partners.

"It's turned off at night. Besides there won't be heating in this little cupboard. Here, have my jacket."

"No, I couldn't."

"Aye, you could."

He's already taken it off and wrapped it around my shoulders. For a moment our eyes lock. I need to do something, anything, to break the silence.

"I w-was w-wondering if I could borrow your coveralls!" I stutter.

He raises both eyebrows. "You're that...cold?" And then he frowns. He has very expressive eyebrows.

I wrap my arms around my middle, stepping away, trying to ignore the heat in my cheeks. "No, you muppet! For tomorrow. For the Christmas party! I know you're a lot taller than me, but I wondered if I could borrow them. Presuming we'll ever get out of here."

His intense stare makes me weak at the knees. Parts of me tingle, parts of me jingle.

"Och, and for a wee while there I was imagining you'd something else entirely in mind." He looks amused. "Shall I take them off now?"

"No! Don't be ridiculous. Forget I even mentioned it!" I squeak. "It was a bloody stupid idea!"

Turning away, I look out of the window, desperately seeking an anchor. Against the square of bruised night, feathers of snow flutter downwards. "Look at that!" Standing on my tiptoes, gripping onto the windowsill, I peer outside. "It's snowing outside, ey? It's settling on the ground too. It's so...I hope we don't get snowed in!"

10

Clyde

She's full of surprises, Miss Hadaway, excited as a kid about snow as if she's never seen snow before, but also there's a tremor of fear in her voice, as if it might be possible for the pair of us to get any more stuck than we already are.

Standing beside her, I take a look outside. It's true, it's picture postcard pretty, the trees and buildings laced in white. In my head, I'm imagining a different story though — Holly and me outside having a snowball fight, building a snowman, going sledging. I wasn't planning to go to the Christmas Party at all. I was put off by the email encouraging staff to dress festive and all the jibes about me getting my kilt on, but now I know Holly's going, even if it is with damn Leo, I'm thinking it might be worth suffering...just to find out what she's planning to do with my coveralls. That makes no sense whatsoever. No matter, I can't miss the opportunity of seeing Holly in her festive finery. My brain is doing cartwheels at the very idea. Not in a kilt though...

We're pitched into darkness for the umpteenth time.

Our hands clash as we both frantically wave to turn the lights on again. These motion-sensor lights are going to be the bloody death of me.

Sitting back down on our respective beanbags, we're bunched together, strewn lopsided, and I start humming Jingle Bells to take my mind off things in my nether regions.

"Jungle bills, jungle bills," she sings alongside me, but stops abruptly when I snort with laughter. "What? It's my accent, ey? In our carol rehearsal earlier, one of the *kuds* started singing Dick the horse, instead of Deck the halls." She annunciates the last phrase with a pucker English accent. "You should've seen Stephanie Dawson's face. Clearly, she thought I was to blame."

I erupt into gales of laughter unable to hold it in any longer. I laugh so hard tears begin to roll down my cheeks.

"What? What's so bloody funny?"

She's priceless. It's not her accent — I love her accent — it's her outraged expression that kills me. I want to pull her into my arms and hug her tight.

"Don't worry about it," I say. "Miss Dawson is just a curmudgeonly spinster."

"A what spinster?"

He smiles ruefully. "Curmudgeonly."

"You can't talk. I bet no-one understands what you're bloody saying most of the time either, with your *wee* this and *och* that and your fancy vocabulary," she mutters, sitting back again, arms folded.

"*Och*, you've nae idea lass," I say. "That's why I'm so sympathetic. We minority folk have to stick together."

She elbows me and grins. "Bloody Scottish muppet."

"Oft, ye bloody Kiwi *eejit*."

"Eejit? Eejit!" she splutters. "Who got us trapped in her in the first place?"

I guess it's my turn to color up nicely.

Chuckling, we settle back into a comfortable silence. For some reason, I feel very at home in this cupboard, more at peace than I have for weeks. Months maybe. I'm beyond caring what my parents think. I'm not quite able to focus on thinking 'poetic' thoughts, but still, I don't feel like it's been an evening wasted. I'd give money to know what Holly is thinking.

"Where did you go to school, Hadaway?" I ask.

It takes her a moment to respond.

"Middle of the wopwops. You'd never have heard of it. What about you?"

I pause. "Scotland," I say. "Also in the wopwops or the Scottish equivalent. You probably won't have heard of it either."

"Try me."

I hesitate. "Gordonstoun."

Her head swivels toward me.

Shite.

"Gordonstoun? As in Gordonstoun, Gordonstoun, where half the bloody British royal family went to school?"

"Och, that's a wee bit of an exaggeration. Only King Charles."

She scrabbles around on the beanbags, almost falling against my chest, but righting herself and pushing away again, as she gawks. "Who are you? Effing Prince Charming?"

"I wish. Wouldn't that be nice. Stuck a closet with Prince Charming. I'm more like the laird of nowhere, but don't take that or my education against me. It's hardly my fault."

Her pained expression relaxes a little. I can guess what she's thinking: how does someone who's been to one of the most elite schools in the UK end up as a groundsman? My parents have asked me the same question, countless times. Not to mention the interrogation I've had about why I chose to take 'time out' from university.

I ask Holly about her past, but she bats my questions back, asking me about what I did after school. Normally, I wouldn't expand on the topic, but for some reason I want to see how she'll react, so I tell her I dropped out of university without going into details of why. Holly goes quiet. I'm all ready for her to flay me, but she just gives my arm a squeeze and falls silent. *Muppet,* I can just about cope with, but this sympathetic silence feels awkward. I feel like I've laid myself bare in front of her, and now, trying not to upset me, she would rather not acknowledge my nakedness. That or she's preoccupied with judging my privileged past.

Conversation seems to have been put in the deep freeze.

The room is pitched into darkness once more, but this time neither of us move.

I hear her soft breathing. She's probably fallen asleep.

The church bells sound in the distance. Midnight already. How the hell did that happen?

I listen to the blood humming around my system. And Holly's childlike breaths. Normally I'd be asleep in an instant, but right now, doused in the claustrophobia of my own lust, making Christmas wishes that can never happen, I lie awake, feeling as if my natural equilibrium has been irrevocably disturbed.

I start to question myself, my life, my whole bloody everything.

What *am* I doing here? Should I go back to university next year? Get a 'proper' job' as my father likes to say only every time he sees me. He likes to remind me I'm throwing my future away. I'm not so sure. I feel content. Right now, I feel extremely content. I'm back to making impossible wishes.

The beanbag makes a whispering sound. The temperature in the room has plummeted and despite my jacket, I can literally hear as well as feel Holly shivering. Should I do something? How can she be asleep?

I stare at her in the silvery light, and, just as I'm worrying about what action I should take, and being extremely indecisive in coming to any sort of rational decision, she rolls toward me, nestling into my chest.

Woah.

I stop breathing altogether. Holly Hadaway gives me heartburn.

Should I ease her away?

Not bloody likely.

This is like the worst sort of physical challenge — her cheek resting in the crook between my chest and my arm, her visibly shivering, me having to resist all my natural impulses.

I wave my hand to see if she's still awake, but she doesn't open her eyes.

I can't help but stare at her tumble of curls, her long dark eyelashes, her petal-smooth skin. She's so fragile. So delicate. Lying back down, I don't want the night to go too fast, loving the caressing touch of her every breath against my neck.

Once the lights go out again, slowly, the beanbag protesting under my shifting weight, telling myself it is the gentlemanly thing to do, I fold my arms around her.

The weak morning sun ruptures the skin of my dreams and I wake with a start, terrified that I've done something untoward. Dreams are just dreams, right? But what if I've inadvertently acted them out in the night. I pray my hands didn't stray in the dark because my imagination seems to have no bounds. At one point, I dreamed I was trying to chain Holly and me together with strips of paper.

Finally, disentangling myself from the beanbags, I peel off my coveralls and try to arrange them over her legs. I pace the cell.

When Holly wakes up, I'm well out of arm's reach, trying to assess her reactions, without making it obvious. She seems unfazed. I'm just about to give her the poem I've spent the wee hours of the morning composing, to distract myself from her (and the fact that my bladder is fit to burst), when a face appears at the stationery door window. Stephanie Dawson.

Holly leaps to her feet, and hastily I stuff the poem in my jeans' pocket.

Mrs Dawson tries the handle, but the door doesn't budge.

"We're locked in!" shouts Holly in my ear.

"Good grief! Have you been in there all night?" Mrs Dawson shouts back.

"Yes. All night! Get us out!" shouts Holly, hastily swiping at the tears which have spilled from her eyes.

Och, man. I want to pull her into my arms again, but as I step toward her, she wards me off.

11

Holly

After an excruciating hour of explanations and shouted instructions, Brian finally appears, and we're released. I'm patted on the back by the kids and staff alike. Clyde gets the hell out of my class as fast as his long legs will take him. During Golden Hour, while the children are busy writing their messages to one another and pasting paper chains together, I'm in my own loop, revisiting last night.

Half awake that morning, I remember having a distinct feeling I'd lost something; I reached out to the person in my dreams, and woke to find the empty space on the beanbags beside me. My heart sank. But then there, leaning against the shelves, stripped down to his jeans and t-shirt, was my beanbag companion, writing again. He does love a bit of composition.

"Morning," I croaked, shuffling up into a sitting position, noticing his coveralls draped across my legs, surreptitiously wiping the dribble from the corner of my mouth.

"Aye, it is that." He looked over and gave me a faint smile, but otherwise his face was inscrutable, a mask of indifference, and any lingering hopes I may have had, any dreamlike fantasies, took a nosedive.

"About last night..." I'd said.

"What about it?"

What about it, Holly? As I help the children to glue paper chains, in my head I'm conducting a full-blown interrogation of myself.

I have no clue what happened to my sense of propriety last night, but it took me hours to get to sleep; I mean properly asleep, not the pretend thing I did when I snuggled into Clyde. In a rash moment, madness had taken ahold. Seeing our breaths mingle freely in the cold night air as we lay on our backs talking, listening to his rumbling belly laugh, I realized I didn't care about where he'd come from, or where he'd been to school, or whether his parents were wealthy or poor, or even what he'd done wrong at university. I'd felt a bit sorry for him, hearing about him supposedly taking time out (reading between the lines he was probably pushed out). There had to be a good reason for that to happen, but he clearly didn't want to spill the tea.

After an hour or so of wishing he would make a move, but him doing diddly squat, I deliberately snuggled in closer and buried my nose in his front. Why? Was it just because I'm lonely? I'm still not sure, but I know he smelled divine. Like a spring day in the park — mown grass, flowerbeds, tall solemn trees.

All I could think about was him lying alongside me, being so careful not to touch. He's a careful man. With careful hands. I like that he's surprising and full of so many contradictions; he's like an unexpected Christmas gift.

It took him forever to put his arms around me, but when he finally did, I fell asleep.

This morning I feel unstuck again. Missing something...or someone.

At recess, I try to get my reports finished, but honestly my brain is scrambled. At recess, I race to the staffroom to grab myself a coffee, only to find most of the teaching staff still chortling as a result of hearing the gossip about my night locked in the stationery storeroom with Clyde. I'm thumped on the back, I'm hugged, my shoulder is squeezed and I'm winked at. They all want to speak to me. Suddenly, I'm everyone's best friend. Their amusement is a little intimidating and a lot embarrassing.

I wish Clyde was around so he could wrap me up in his arms again. I can't help thinking a couple of the female staff look slightly aggrieved, as if they wish it had been them, not me, stuck with Clyde.

Calmly, casually I hope, I deflect questions as I finish making my brew.

I catch drift of one bit of gossip that I seem to have been unaware of all term: Was I the only member of staff who didn't know Clyde is something of a minor celebrity? It's a bit of a shock to learn that he's a published poet. A man of words, though as far as I could gather from last night, he uses them very economically. A man who, according to staffroom gossip, has walked away from his place at Oxford University to slum it in coveralls and pursue his dreams of writing.

I listen to the other better-informed members of staff, feeling utterly, increasingly, totally stupid. "How is this the first time I've heard of it?" I ask.

'Well, what do you expect? You're always so head in the clouds and busy being busy," says Stephanie, nudging me with a sharp elbow. "So did Burtonbridge's Poet Laureate *pin* you a sonnet?"

Ha, bloody ha! Now she chooses to joke. "No, of course he didn't *pen* me a sonnet!" I snap, wishing he had.

Oops from the look on her face, I've overstepped the mark. "Sorry, I'm tired." Tired of her correcting my accent as if the only way to speak English is with a punnet full of plums in your mouth.

She looks thoroughly *miffed*, as she would put it. "Not too tired to get those reports sent this morning, I hope." She widens her eyes and gives a little disappointed shake of her head.

"I'm on to it right now," I say, happy to have an excuse to leave the staffroom.

Back in my classroom, my computer is miraculously working again, the snow blizzard dispersed. Nevertheless, I spend ten minutes staring at the monitor screen, not able to focus at all. All I can see is

Clyde's face; all I can hear is his voice. My computer is now functional, but my brain is broken. In the end, I send Stephanie the reports as they are. If all I have to suffer is some of Stephanie's 'I'm sick and tired of correcting everyone's errors', I'll just have to grin and bear it.

At lunchtime I'm on duty outside, walking around the perimeter of the school grounds, trying to suck some fresh air and common sense into my lungs, when I spot Clyde strolling across the upper terrace. I can't help wishing I'd noticed him weeks ago. He looks in my direction, and I raise a hand to wave, but he veers sharply left, disappearing into the school building.

"Miss Hadaway!"

My hand falls back to my side, and I look around feeling foolish and deflated. One of the kids has tripped and barked his shin. "Oh no, Henry. Poor you." It's not bad, but he's wailing. After calming him down, I instruct Bertie to accompany him and send them off to the school nurse. I wish I could go with them. I need fixing. I feel raw, like my heart has been barked.

The outside bell finally clangs to signal end of lunch recess and I trudge back to my classroom. The children are already lined up outside, waiting to be let in, but I need a moment to compose myself.

"Give me one more minute," I say, with a rigor-mortis smile, shutting the door behind me.

Placing my jacket on the back of my chair, I head for the stationery room. All I want to do is to sink into the beanbag and whimper in the dark, but somehow I have to pull myself together and get through the afternoon.

I spot Clyde's coveralls in a heap beside the bean bags. Why didn't he take them with him? Surely he must have needed them today? Without thinking, I pick them up and press them against my burning face.

Images from last night, cutting those slips of paper, him writing his words, me practically throwing myself at him on the beanbags, return with a vengeance. He'd done nothing more than hold me in his arms because I was cold. What must he have thought of me though? *Desperate*! I sniff. *Daggy*! And sniff again. What had he called me? *Eejit!* Not much poetic about that! I close my eyes. There's a lingering scent of Clyde. I inhale even more deeply, recalling how good it felt to be with him.

The inside bell rings for the start of the next lesson. Okay, sniffing Clyde's overalls is a little obsessive. Get a grip, Hadaway!

Stifling a groan, I blow my nose and straighten my shoulders.

I have to do this. I am a teacher. I am a professional. I have standards to uphold, and I more to the point, I haven't dragged my sorry backside all the way from New Zealand for nothing. I'm not about to give up now. I just have to make it through to the end of the week… and then I can collapse in a heap.

"In you come," I say, cheerful smile glued in place as I open the classroom door. Resolutely, I head back to my desk, but something makes me look up. A paper chain garland hangs on the wall behind my desk; I definitely didn't put that one all the way up there. That would take someone with long arms.

The children stream back into the classroom, clamoring for my attention. I sneak glances at the paper hoops dangling above the board behind my desk in full view of everyone. There's something very familiar about the handwriting — enough to make me trip over my own chair so the children squeal with laughter.

"You and your *big* feet!" says Charlie.

"Yes, alright Charlie. Simmer down."

12

Clyde

Even though I'm not looking at her, even though she's lying right there, I can't stop replaying the scene from the moment I woke up: Holly and Holly and Holly in my head. She'd looked so beautiful in the mauve of the morning. So vulnerable. Hair splayed. Legs askew. Fresh faced and untouched. I wanted to keep her locked in my arms forever, but I was also rendered breathless...with lust. There was no way I could keep lying next to her, feeling myself become increasingly aroused. It could only prove humiliating. Not to mention inappropriate.

I had eased myself from the beanbag and started writing, feeling for the words in the dim light, hoping they would hit their mark and keep me from contemplating...other things.

And then with no warning, there was a squawk from outside, some rapping on the wood and Mrs Dawson's startled face appeared at the window of the door.

The spell was broken.

As to be expected, the other grounds' staff take great delight in ribbing me all morning.

What kind of motorbike would Clyde like for Christmas? A Holly Davison.

What does Clyde get after a night stuck in a teacher's cupboard? Holly wood.

If Clyde has to go to hospital because of a broken heart, what Christmas carol would the doctors sing to get him better? The Holly and the I.V.

It's typical boys' banter and doesn't get any better as the day progresses. As best I can, I block it out and get on with emptying leaves from the various gutters around the school, but as I work my head bustles with images and words fighting for space and air — or *ear* as Holly would say. Every thought of her brings the smile back to my lips. Yes, perhaps pursuing her might lead to humiliation, but when I spot her outside at lunchtime, something snaps: there's no way I can leave it at this.

I steal back into her stationery store, hastily write out a message, and leave my paper chain of words tacked on the wall behind her desk where she can't miss it. It's a paper chain of promises and hopes. An invitation as fragile as a daisy chain.

Okay, it's no Dear Santa letter, but maybe my Christmas wishes will be granted:

Dear Santa, please, I'd like a sprig of Holly in my Christmas stocking...

13

Holly

All afternoon I fidget like crazy, distracted by the paper chain stuck on the classroom wall. Anticipation makes my heart race and I lose track of what I'm saying to the children dozens of times. For them it's an afternoon of fits of giggles; for me, it's an afternoon of torture. I try to look serious and frown, but for some reason it doesn't have its usual effect. I'm too tired even to be angry.

I count down the hours and minutes until the final school bell, pacing the classroom floor, throwing furtive glances at the paper chain, almost pushing the children out the classroom door when it's time for them to go home.

As soon as they've left, I close the door, race back to my desk, and pulling my chair over to the wall, stand on it to take down Clyde's paper chain.

His words take my breath away.

Link breath, link limbs, link words and life,
Open your lips and silently purr.

Be rapt in our paper chains.
On a stationery date.
With me, tonight.
Lock it
In.

x

I hope to God it means what I think it might mean. But does it? Am I reading too much into it? I'm supposed to be the teacher for goodness sake, but I have no idea. Now who's the muppet? I thought I liked poetry. I *know* I like Clyde. But does this mean I should meet him here tonight? But tonight's the staff Christmas party! That can't be right.

And, oh hell, I still haven't sorted my outfit.

Of course, I take myself to the stationery cupboard for a quick scream. And there on the floor, I catch sight of his green coveralls again. I could make use of those tonight. Maybe all is not lost.

Looking at my watch, I realize I only have a couple of hours to get home, showered and return here, dressed for action.

My heart patters in my chest as I drive home. I want to hit the gas, but the snow and ice on the road looks treacherous. I try to focus on driving, but how can I with all the questions still bubbling away in my brain? It's not entirely clear. I could be misinterpreting Clyde's words. Does he mean meet him before the party, during or afterwards? When exactly? Couldn't he have written something a bit more explicit like, *Meet me in here at 9.30pm?* What if I'm reading more into it than he intended? In the classroom, I read his paper chain message over and over again, but now I begin to doubt it's even written by him..

By the time I've dashed into town, found a large amount of tinsel, a Christmas hat, a mustache and beard, and, best of all, a pair of Star Trek Dr Spock ears I spotted in the newsagents, I've less than an hour to sort myself out. I want to look my best not like the bedraggled wreck I was this morning.

I'm so nervous my hands shake as I get myself dressed in my

sexiest underwear, telling myself red lace is just another festive touch and no-one, except myself, will be seeing it...

I pull Clyde's green coveralls over the top, roll up the hems of the sleeves and legs and cinch it all in with a red leather belt. To top it off, I add the beard and Dr Spock ears. I'm not sure I'll pass as an elf, but at least I won't be criticized for lack of effort.

My heart begins to hammer a little at the thought of Clyde's long limbs inside these garments the night before. His words run on repeat in my head. *Link breath, link limbs, link words and life. Open your lips and silently purr.* I purr at my reflection in the mirror. *It's not very sexy at all. Be rapt in our paper chains. On a stationery date.* Stationary or stationery?

What the heck. I may be confused and a little bit deluded, but there's no harm in being hopeful.

My mad curls are way too untamed to be considered 'elfish', but this could be worse. My face is flushed. Why wouldn't it be? I believe, at least I dare to *hope*, that Clyde and I bonded last night. He'd left me a clear (if slightly open to interpretation) message by sticking his paper chain invitation above my desk. I have slept in his arms and I can't wait to be back in them. I like everything about him from his steady hands to his unsteadying eyes, not to forget his Scottish lilt and way with words. Perhaps he liked me too — was that impossible to believe? I press the back of my hands against my cheeks. They are hot enough to barbecue on, but at least my beard and mustache hide a multitude of sinful thoughts.

Perhaps tonight will be the icing on the Christmas cake, the angel on top of the tree, the answer to all my Christmas dreams and wishes.

Clyde Hunter and I have a date of sorts — I know roughly where, I'm just not exactly sure of when.

14

Clyde

When I get home from school at the end of the day, who do I find waiting for me outside my house? Olivia, my childhood friend and ex-girlfriend. She looks sleek and manicured as ever stepping out of her silver Porsche onto the sidewalk. When did she ever not look fabulous? Being manicured is kind of a full time occupation for her. But either she's had a little too much botox injected into her lips lately, or her pouting has become even more pronounced since I last saw her.

"Clyde, finally! I've been waiting forever!" She stamps her feet and flicks her hair over her shoulders. "What happened to you last night? Where on earth were you?"

"Hello, Olivia. What an unexpected…surprise," I say, when she pauses for breath.

"We were worried sick when you didn't show or answer your phone. Your parents had to leave for London, so I promised I'd check in on you for them."

"Right." Damn! I'd spent all day thinking about Holly and forgotten to call mum to apologize for my no-show the previous evening. Not that they could have been that concerned; they'd gone off to London this morning without it troubling their conscience too much.

"Oh, darling, never mind them. Our folks can be such bores. I'm not here to give you a ticking off. But seriously, how are you? It's been such a long time since I saw you last, darling, and you never call. I do miss you, you know. Oxford's not the same without you at all, darling. You really must consider coming back. I have to say, Marjorie and Hamish are in total agreement about that. You're simply wasting a wonderful opportunity."

"Did you tell them?" I ask.

"About what?" She manages to look nonchalant.

"You know what," I growl.

She immediately puts my back up even though I should be used to it by now. This is Liv's usual barrage of charm and giving me grief. I'd almost forgotten how she simultaneously manages to amuse me, exasperate me and make me feel like an absolute sod. Dating her was a perpetual rollercoaster. A real mistake. Liv's not deliberately difficult or inconsiderate. She's been a close friend of mine since we were little more than tadpoles and I'm sure I've done worse than stand her up for dinner before…I seem to remember feeding her dog food once and telling her it was paté. And she's done worse to me. Much worse. But she acts as if it's all long forgotten and we've put our differences behind us.

It's surreal seeing her here in Burtonbridge. Out of whack. This place is not exactly a thriving metropolis. There has to be a reason. If our parents think they can push us back together again, they are very much mistaken.

Liv needs someone who can keep her in the manner to which she's accustomed — the sort of manner that requires a hefty bank balance, and a pandering boyfriend who's prepared to turn a blind eye to her indiscretions. As it turns out, I'm neither: my father has informed me my inheritance would not be forthcoming since I gave up my place at Oxford, which is a relief because I don't want to be beholden to anyone, least of all him; and as for turning a blind eye, I prefer to live life with my eyes open thank you kindly.

Dutifully, I kiss her on both cheeks. "Thanks for checking in. I'm fine. Have you been here long?"

"Only the whole day! Not that you'd care," she replies arching her eyebrows. "I couldn't even get a manicure. All booked up, can you believe it? Here! To occupy myself, I went for a little browse around the shops, all four of them, while I was waiting. Oh, stop looking so exasperated. I thought the town was rather quaint actually. I even discovered a boutique dress shop selling Galliano. Here in...where are we again?"

"Burtonbridge. Imagine that. You finding a dress shop you liked. How very fortunate."

"Liked is putting it a little too strongly, but it wasn't bad. Oh stop looking so...so...irascible!" She rolls her eyes and hits my arm.

"Irascible? You must have been attending lectures. What a reformation. I'm impressed."

"Clyde," — She flares her pert nostrils at me — "stop teasing. You know I don't like it. Behave! I was pleasantly surprised there's life up here in the north of England, that's all."

I smile ruefully. "More than you could possibly imagine. Look, my phone's run out of juice and I've only just made it home after a long day at work."

"Oh yes?" She raises her manicured brows.

"It's a long story."

"A long interesting story...from what I heard...Is it true you got stuck in a cupboard with one of the female teachers?" She snickers like a horse behind her hand.

My eyes narrow. "How did you hear about...?" I trail off not wanting to give her any information she doesn't already know.

"I knew there had to be an explanation for your no-show. I mean, okay, we're no longer engaged, but it's not like you'd stand me up deliberately or go out of your way to avoid me, or our parents. Marjorie and Hamish were understandably disappointed though, and last night was incredibly awkward."

"Is that your excuse for not telling them?"

She ignores my dig. "I think your papa was hoping you'd reconsider your current situation. Imagine his reaction when I explain his son was simply stuck a cupboard with a female member of staff when he was supposed to be fixing her lock." Her laughter jars.

I smile a little wearily. "I'd appreciate it if you didn't go into details. I'll explain myself when I next see him."

She watches me unlock the front door. "You sure nothing happened?"

You could be forgiven for thinking she's jealous, but I know better. Liv is simply one of those girls who has to be foremost in every man's mind. "Nothing happened. There's nothing to gossip about and nothing to tell my parents. If I could've got out of there, I would've done. End of." Even as I'm saying this, I'm thinking to myself what a big fat lie it is. It wasn't nothing. I can't wait to repeat the experience. If Holly does a no-show tonight, I'll be gutted. I need to get Liv off my back, but it's like she has a sixth sense about these things.

"If you say so…" She doesn't sound convinced. "You know what our parents are like. They can't help hoping—"

"Pushing. Pushing us together."

"Is that so very dreadful?" She looks hurt.

Yes, actually, the very idea fills me with total dread. "I enjoy your company, Liv, you know I do. I'm fond of you, but after everything that's happened between us…We're never going to be more than friends. You know that."

She blinks at me. Her eyes are glassy. She purses her lips and I feel like I've been a little too blunt. If she's truly a friend, I can't very well send her away in tears. Oh sod it.

"You coming in?" I ask, regretting it almost immediately when her pouting mouth transforms into an immediate beaming smile.

"Absolutely!" she says, wiping her Louboutin-heeled feet gingerly on the doormat. "This way? Up here?"

"Aye."

She leads the way up the darkened stairwell, giving me an eyeful of her shapely behind.

I squeeze past her to unlock the door to my attic flat inhaling her familiar, heady perfume. I throw my keys on the kitchen counter.

"Oh. My. God!" she says, wrinkling her nose as she steps inside, with shock written large on her face. "You've taken the whole garret thing to heart, haven't you, darling? Why are you living in such miserable mouse hole?" She looks around with undisguised horror. "This is worse than student digs. My God! No wonder the cupboard wasn't a problem. No wonder you need cheering up."

"Says who?"

"Marjorie."

I exhale heavily. Marjorie, my mother, cannot imagine me being happy living anywhere other than in a castle in Scotland.

"The two of us had a bit of a chinwag last night."

I bet they did. "I know she doesn't like where I'm living, but if I'd returned to Scotland I'd have had my folks breathing down my neck. I happen to like my mouse hole." Although, right now, I feel a bit like the cat has crept inside.

"And what about Oxford? Don't you miss it at all?"

What she means is don't I miss her. I can hardly tell her that I'm relieved to be rid of her. Here, I have air and can breathe. "I needed a fresh start. I'm happy though, seriously, so feel free to report that back to Ma. I like it here. Why don't you think of it as bijoux rather than mouse hole." I smile ruefully.

She shudders. "Bijoux is not a word I like unless it's jewelry."

I shrug. There's nothing wrong with this studio apartment. It may only be one room, but I like the dormer windows that look over the Burtonbridge rooftops. Right now, they're decorated white with snow and smoke rises lazily from its chimneys. Beyond the town are the wooded hills, and the school on the top of the hill. Which reminds me, I need to get ready for tonight.

"Tea?" I ask, trying to assume an air of nonchalance, so she doesn't cotton on that I have plans. How to get rid of her, without making her feel unwanted and unappreciated.

"Tea?" she repeats, a hurt look returning to her eyes.

I open the fridge. "Or beer?"

"Beer! Don't you have any wine at least?"

I sigh and open an overhead cupboard. I pull out a bottle of whiskey.

"How about this?"

"I suppose...a wee dram."

As I pour us both a small measure, I can't help thinking this could all go wrong all too easily, like a car losing its grip in snow. Our relationship was a bit like that. One minute we were good friends, and the next second we were dating, and then...How quickly she seems to have forgotten it was her who did the dirty on me and had an affair with someone else, when we were purportedly engaged. How easily she seems to have wiped the memory of me catching them in bed together. I haven't told my parents those little details despite the temptation — just to get them off my back.

"So, Liv. Are you going to tell me who've you been talking to and how you found out about my cupboard affair? You know you could have rung school to check where I was."

"I certainly hope it wasn't an affair!" She sits down on the end of my bed and gives it a little bounce to test it. She looks up and gives an embarrassed little smile as if she knows she's been caught in the act of doing something naughty. "Fine. If you say so, it wasn't an affair or anything of that nature. It was an accident. I guess I just needed some time to absorb the news and some reassurance. I was a bit... upset to be honest. It was the shock finding out you might be dating another woman already. I knew it was going to happen sooner or later, I just hoped it might be later..."

For a minute, I say nothing. I'm figuring out how to play this. Sticking to the lie seems to be the best option. "Like I said, it was nothing. One night stuck in a cupboard with a Kiwi is not a date. It didn't mean a thing." Lies. Lies. Lies. It means everything.

Her eyes latch onto mine, and I look away. "Clyde, I wasn't born yesterday. I can see it means more than you're letting on."

"Don't be daft. I'm just tired." Arms folded, I stare out the window wondering what Holly is up to now, who Liv found out from and how I'm going to get rid of her. Perhaps, the silence will speak for itself.

"In case you're wondering, my day was quite entertaining actually," she says. "I literally bumped into this very hot bloke wearing rugby kit...Amazing thighs." She clears her throat. "Leo, he said his name was. He was the person who told me what had happened to you. He seemed to think it was hilarious."

Bloody Leo shouldn't think it was hilarious. If anyone should be outraged, it was him.

"He also mentioned there was a staff party at your school tonight and staff were free to invite guests..."

Nooo! Inwardly, I groan.

"So - ohh." She draws it out expectantly. "Have you invited anyone?"

I sigh. "I'm not going."

"Not going to your staff party? That's ludicrous!"

"For God's sake, why don't you just be honest with me. You're going with this Kiwi, aren't you?"

I groan out loud. "No, I'm not."

"But she's special to you?"

I knock back the rest of my whiskey. "Aye, if you really want to know the truth, I think she could be. I'd like her to be. But actually I think she's rather smitten with your man, Leo."

Her chin goes back. That shocked her. "Oh. Really? The plot thickens," she says, a small smile playing around her lips. She pours both of us another dram of whiskey.

"No more for me," I say.

"So you are going to the staff party. I knew it. Well, don't mind me. I'll find something to occupy myself with. I can make a few phone calls..."

I'm reminded of her threat to talk to my parents. "How's it you're so very interested in my social life all of a sudden? Have my parents put you up to this?"

"Not at all! I'm your friend. And as your friend, I'm also interested in your welfare...and I'd like to help make amends for the past. I'm booked in to the hotel until tomorrow, so you'd best make use of me."

My eyes narrow. "Amends how?"

She avoids my eyes. "You know. I didn't want to hurt you. Not for too long anyhow," she says, pouting. "I regret how things turned out. Things just sort of went awry."

"Awry. Right."

Turning away from me, she bends to open my fridge and inspect the contents. "I'm not proud of what I did, Clyde. If I could turn back the clock, I would."

"You *did* more than once. You'd break the bloody clock."

"Don't you have anything healthy to eat? You need to take care of yourself. A good diet is terribly important." When she looks back at me over her shoulder, her cheeks are flushed despite the fact that she's had her head in my fridge.

"I don't see how you can make amends now. I'm not going back to the way we were. I've moved on. I thought you had too."

"Yes, I have, I have…But more than anything, I want us to be friends again." She twiddles a long strand of hair around her finger. "I think you might be the only true friend I ever had."

The problem with Liv is that she wants to control and charm and bewitch every man she comes across. She needs to feel attractive. She is attractive, but if I ever was attracted to her, I'm no longer under her spell. But once upon a time, she was a good friend. If only we had stuck to that.

Our first term at Oxford, we'd clung to each other's company and after one too many drinks our 'friendship' had got out of hand. For a while I was swept along by her enthusiasm.

One mad night, she'd suggested what a perfect couple we'd make and how delighted our parents would be. Drunkenly, I agreed. The next thing I knew, a week later, before we'd even told anyone we were dating, she had informed our parents we were engaged. I was stunned. The whole situation had snowballed nightmarishly out of control even though I knew, almost immediately, that it didn't feel right. While I was trying to figure out a way to extract myself from the whole hideous scenario and not hurt a girl who'd been a friend my whole life, I caught Liv in bed with one of my mates.

At the time, she was outraged, as was I, only for very different reasons. For a while, I'd been very confused and angry. But looking back, with the benefit of hindsight, I can now see it gave us the ideal get-out of marriage clause. She wasn't really the type to be faithful to one man, and I was almost grateful for her indiscretion. One of the reasons I'd left Oxford was to make a clean break for both of us and to get my head straight.

But she had promised to come clean with our parents and last night would have provided the perfect opportunity.

Suddenly, here and now, I am very clear how I feel. Pissed off.

"Liv, look, it's a shame things didn't work out between us, but we both know that was for the best. We need to find people we want to spend the rest of our lives with, without straying—"

"I know! I'm fine. I'm over it. Believe it or not, I'm over you! I'm just trying to help."

I resist rolling my eyes. "Really?"

"Yes, really! Wouldn't it be fun to go to your Christmas party together. It would be like the good old days before we hooked up. Perhaps I could even distract Leo's attention from this girl of yours. I think he was attracted to me." She attempts to look coy. "I have to admit, I thought he was rather hot..." She catches herself and stops mid-sentence. "Unless, you think this other friend of yours is serious about him. So what's she called?"

"Holly." I know I shouldn't be Machiavellian, but something about Liv's plan strikes a chord. Maybe Holly will realize Leo's not right for her, in the same way as I have realized Liv definitely wasn't right for me. Was that completely immoral?

Of course, at the end of the day or evening Holly would be free to make her own decision, but I really can't see Leo making her happy. "I need to think about this. I need to get ready. I haven't had a shower since the day before yesterday—"

"I did wonder about the aroma. Need me to scratch your back? Only metaphorically speaking!" She winks.

I roll my eyes.

"You know how I love a party," says Liv. "The very least I can do is make you look good. It'll be awful for you to have to turn up alone."

She wrinkles her nose. "If you want me to come with you, you'd better make your mind up fast. I can't just be ready in five seconds flat like you, you know."

For a second, I'm dumbfounded. I've forgotten how Liv manages to manipulate every situation to suit herself. But perhaps she's genuinely keen on Leo, because a school party is about the last place Olivia would usually show her face. "Liv, you'll hate it. You don't have to do this for me."

"Nonsense. I'd be delighted. It'll be fun. I have a lion to tame!" She grins wickedly like she's the circus ringmaster.

I don't believe it. She's after Leo. "Well, in that case…I suppose—"

"I'll go and fetch my bag. You don't mind me showering first, do you?" asks Liv. She comes and stands in front of me, clasping the front of my shirt. "We'll have a blast tonight. Knock the socks off everyone else. Show them a bit of style. Besides, I've been waiting all day to spend some time with you, you can't seriously expect me to turn tail and head straight back to Oxford. I've already bought a heavenly cocktail dress for the occasion…"

She sweeps out and downstairs.

A couple of hours later, not letting go of my arm, Olivia sashays into the school Christmas party as if she owns the place and everyone is there for her own amusement. Looking svelte in a slinky backless red cocktail dress, she's on top form. Flirtatious. Bubbly. Possibly coked-up. I was going to go in casual jeans and a shirt, but she's insisted I wear my kilt, and I didn't resist too hard as a little bit of me secretly hopes it will impress Holly.

Entering the main hall where the party is being held, I'm a bag of nerves and take a back seat while Olivia regales everyone with stories from university. I scan the room for any sign of Holly, only half-listening.

Suddenly there's a commotion by the front door, as someone trips and lurches into the room. Ho bloody ho, it could only be Holly because I'd recognize those baby blue eyes anywhere, and those are my green coveralls. Only now, as she's looking around the room looking lost, do I twig why she wanted to borrow them. The poor lass has come in fancy dress. But as what? A Christmas tree? A green goblin? A bearded Martian? I've no idea, but I'm grinning from ear to ear by the time she spots me.

Holly takes a few hesitant steps in my direction, before Liv grabs hold of my arm and hisses in my ear, "That's not *our* Holly, is it?"

"No, that is *my* Holly," I growl, feeling inexplicably possessive.

"Holly and the Highlander," says Liv, and starts to giggle.

15

Holly

I'm late to the staff Christmas party, and I can hear the pumping beat of music before I even step a foot inside the door. Unfortunately, it's not until I've tripped over the threshold into the room that my bubble of excitement deflates like a popped balloon — I'm the only muppet in fancy dress. Seriously. The only one.

I scan the room. *Bugger! Bugger! Bugger it!* Everyone else is dressed very *fancy*, but not fancy-dressed. For a heart-lifting moment, I spot Clyde and think, oh good, he's come in fancy dress as a Highlander. He's wearing a kilt and I'm ready to be swept off my feet. But then, a stunning red-head takes his arm and whispers in his ear. She's looking directly at me and laughing her beautiful head off — at least, I wish it would drop off. And then I recall that a kilt would not be considered fancy dress for someone who's actually Scottish.

Thank God for the beard, so no-one can see how embarrassed I am. I think of removing it, but it's too late now, everyone has seen me. Instead, yanking it higher so it covers more of my face, wishing I could vanish in a fancy puff of smoke, I make a beeline for the bar.

Clyde's date looks as if she's stepped off the red carpet at the

Oscars. All that grooming. All that *coiffeuring*. That dazzling bling. I suspect she could be wearing more than a year's worth of my salary around her neck. And to top it off Clyde is still laughing. Maybe the paper chain was some sort of sick joke. Maybe I misinterpreted the whole thing. Maybe I am going to get very drunk.

Grabbing a glass of wine, and no doubt looking like some sort of evil pantomime dame, I lift my beard and drain the glass, before surreptitiously reaching for another.

"Woah! Ghostbusters!" says Leo Tarrant coming to stand beside me. He starts singing the annoying theme tune from the film. "Nice coveralls."

Oh piss off, Leo, I think, until out of the corner of my eye I lock eyes with Clyde again, still grinning. Remembering my lie from the night before, I put my drink down, clamp my hands around the back of Leo's neck and plant a smacker of a kiss on his lips. "Merry Christmas, Leo!"

He recoils, but luckily for me he has his back to Clyde. I'm not sure he was expecting that kiss, let alone the face full of beard, and I've left remnants of white fluff on his designer stubble. "Bloody hell, woman, steady on!"

Before he can protest or beat a retreat, I grab his bicep in a pincer grip and stare meaningfully into his startled eyes. "Leo, you've been making inappropriate comments to me all term. You owe me one. And I do not mean just that kiss. Have no fear, the real me does not fancy you in the slightest, but we're having a dance."

"Oh."

"Yes. Maybe several. Let's see if you have any coordination off the sports pitch."

"I'm sure I do. I've been told—"

Not listening, I drag poor Leo into the middle of the dance floor. To say I dance my butt off is an understatement. I dance as if I am on the Titanic and have been told this is my last night. I dance as if I am Beyoncé's choreographer. I dance as if I am married to Fred Astaire… only not quite so gracefully because the hem of Clyde's coveralls keeps unrolling and tripping me up.

Unfortunately, at some point, while I'm re-rolling my errant trouser cuffs, Leo slips my grasp.

I spot him talking to Clyde and his date. What a traitor! Leo was meant to be with me. Well, in some figment of my imagination. And now all three of them are laughing and looking at me as if I'm the entertainment for the night. *Damn the whole lot of them!* I refuse to think about what they might be discussing. Clyde, the beguiling bastard (looking unfairly handsome in that kilt) thinks he can beckon me over to join their little cackling trio. What so I can be the butt of even more jokes? *No thanks, mate!*

I pretend like I haven't seen him, just like he did to me at lunchtime. I am so stupid. Why didn't I read the signs when he ignored me then? How can I have misinterpreted this situation so badly? Not to mention the dress code. If there was ever a definition of muppet, the name Holly Hadaway must be written next to it.

At the bar, I attempt to avoid conversation, only to realize I'm surrounded by Clyde's groundsmen colleagues.

"Ho, ho, ho!" I say, raising my glass and taking an enormous gulp.

"So, stationery lock's still not fixed, I gather," says Brian looking earnest. "Sorry about that."

"Maybe I'll put in a request to Santa. Might happen a bit quicker."

George Michael is crooning, *Last Christmas*.

"Knock, knock," says Brian, trying to fill the awkward silence.

"Who's there?" another man obliges.

"Holly."

Oh hell's bells, we're onto bad jokes already

"Holly who?"

"Hollelujah!" I shout before anyone else can get in a punch line.

"I like that!"

"Good one!"

The men laugh and I neck my glass of wine.

Someone clears their throat nervously. "What do you call—"

"A Scotsman who can't fix a door lock?" I ask.

They look at one another perplexed.

"Clyde. It's not a joke," I say narrowing my eyes and turning on

Brian. "Why don't you tell me a bit more about your friend, Clyde?" I'm hoping they'll dish the dirt on him, but they go all insipid and nice.

"He's a good bloke."

"Works hard."

"A grafter."

"Always willing to take one for the team."

I sigh. "Oh, come one, pull the other one. You make him sound like a saint." I flap my beard around. "Can you imagine what his school reports were like? Could try harder. A tendency to waste time. Thinks he's pulled the wool over the teacher's eyes but…he hasn't. He must have some flaws!" I look at the ceiling decorations, blinking hard. What has got into me?

"Well, he's Scottish," says one.

That's the best they can do.

I snort with derisive laughter and wipe my eyes with the end of my beard.

Brian pats my arm.

"Listen, I think…I know it's none of my business but…"

Do they know it's Christmas starts playing and Brian's voice fades into the background. Looking down, I realize my beard has slipped and is now hanging around my neck as if I've grown chest-hair. "Could be worse. Happy Christmas, guys," I say and weave my way back to the dance floor.

I spend the rest of the evening with one eye on Clyde, deliberately moving in an opposite direction whenever he comes toward me. It's like a game of cat and mouse. The night gathers pace, spinning into fast forward mode. And genuinely spinning, because I do a lot of dancing and a lot of drinking. I concentrate my efforts on pretending to have super fun, doing my best Holly-Golightly impression.

When the slow music starts, and Mariah Carey sings *All I want for Christmas is you*, I finally look around for Clyde. I can't believe it's already the end of the party. The room has thinned out. Most people have gone home. Doing a staggering pirouette, I realize that includes Clyde, his date and Leo. Clyde's really gone. How very depressing.

They must have left when I was making a fool of myself, and I could have gone home instead of keeping up this ridiculous charade. Fool. Muppet. Loser. I'm so angry with myself. With the whole world.

"Bloody incompetent nitwit!" I growl, whirling around, slapping straight into the headmaster's chest.

He steps backwards, forehead creased, grabbing my arms. "Steady on. Oh, Holly, I hope you've had a pleasant evening. May I say, I thought you were terribly brave coming dressed as a gnome. By the way, your school reports—"

"Excuse me," I say, cutting him short, before he can say any more. "I've got a lady emergency!"

Friendly huddles of staff are leaving, blocking the exit, saying lengthy goodbyes. Realizing I'll never keep it together and make it out of the front door without someone spotting me in tears, I flee instead for the exit which leads toward my classroom. Like Cinderella in a pinball machine, I hurtle between the last swaying couples, stumbling as fast as I can from the hall. The cooler air hits me, sobering me up a little.

What on earth am I doing in England when I could be teaching in New Zealand? What sort of desperate idiot am I hankering after an adventure and ending up on the other side of the planet from my family and friends? Why am I spending Christmas by myself, when I could have spent it with the people I love?

16

Clyde

The door to the stationery storeroom flies opens and Holly lurches in.

"What the...!"

"Finally!" I lumber to my feet. I've been in here for at least an hour, biding my time, gluing another long string of paper chains together, praying against the odds that Holly will show up even though she's been studiously steering clear of me all evening.

"What are you doing here? Where's your date? That woman?" she asks, wiping her eyes with the back of her hand, unable to disguise the fact that her mascara has left inky trails down her cheeks and white beard.

"With yours." My mouth twists into a smile. "Leo and Liv seem to have hit it off. I hope you don't mind too much. I really couldn't care less where they've gone."

"Oh. But I was never...I thought..."

"Yes, Leo explained the situation. And Liv's an old family friend."

"Oh. A very beautiful friend."

"Not as stunning as you tonight. You were spectacular." I take her hand and pull her closer.

"I was a spectacle, not spectacular. And maybe stunned." She looks doubtful and her chin wobbles. I'm guessing she's also a bit pie-eyed.

"I was ridiculous. It was hollible. *Hollible!*" Even her laugh is wobbly.

"Spectacular. Stunning. Very green," I murmur, looking down at her and smiling.

"I like how you roll your rrrrrrs," she replies, trying to roll hers and failing. She touches my lips with her finger and I almost lose it.

I slowly, begin to ravel the paper garlands I've made around her shoulders.

"I'm not a bloody Christmas tree you know." She hiccups.

"Och, I wasn't sure. What is it you're meant to be exactly?"

"I'm an elf!" She thumps me on the chest. "One of Santa's little helpers. The kids would've known."

"For sure, they would. They're probably a whole lot smarter than me."

"Yes, Oxford boy!" she says accusingly.

"Not anymore."

Suddenly, she throws her arms around my middle and hugs me tight. "Why didn't you say anything, when I was banging on about books? You've clearly read twice as many, three times, maybe ten times as many as me."

"I don't know about *tin* times..."

"Oh, shut up! Why didn't you come and save me tonight? I've spent the entire evening making a muppet of myself."

"Hold on, I thought I was the muppet."

"You are!"

"Would you have liked me to fan the flames of school gossip?"

She pouts. "Your colleagues couldn't stop being nice about you. They seemed to think you're a saint."

I laugh. "Hmmm. I don't honestly care what *they* think."

"That's what I like about you. You don't care what anyone thinks of you. You're just yourself."

"I do. I care what *some* people think. I care a lot about what you think. There's an awful lot you don't know about me."

"And there's plenty you don't know about me too," she says.

"Liv is just a friend. Perhaps bringing her tonight was a big mistake."

She closes her mouth and frowns. "You think?" She elbows me. "Well. I suppose I'm always telling the kids to learn from their mistakes."

I squeeze her hand in mine. "I've learned what I want...from life."

She gazes up intently at me. "And what's that?"

"To start with, I'd like to spend time with you. I've been counting on us having time to find out more about each other. In fact, I'd like to spend a whole a lot of time getting to know Holly Hadaway a lot better...so...What are your plans for Christmas?" I can't believe those words have slipped from my mouth. My paper chain wrapping has come to a stop. What if she bolts?

"You want to spend Christmas with me?"

"Aye. If not in this cupboard, I thought I could find us a wee bolt-hole in Scotland as far away from other folks as possible." Placing my hands on her shoulders, I stare down at her red-rimmed, mascara smeared eyes. "All I want is for Christmas is right here, Holly."

"I have a bit of a stationery fetish as well..."

I roar with laughter. To my mind, she couldn't look any more gorgeous than she does with her soggy beard and mascara streaked face dressed in green coveralls. My emotions threaten to boil over. "You could be an alien from outer space for all I care. A bank robber. A crook. A goddamn prickly pear tree, and I'd still want to spend time with you. Starting tonight. And hopefully the night after that. Who cares, as long as we're together. Do you think you could bear to lower your standards and spend some time with me?"

Watching her smile is better than watching the town's Christmas light being switched on. "Lower my standards? Ha! That'll be a first."

I pull her toward the bean bags.

"I've spent the last hour writing an ode to my green overalls. Would you like to hear?" I ask.

"Yuppie! Of course, I do!" she says adorably, giving me a shove. "I want to hear all your poems. All your stories. In fact, I'd like to hear you recite the encyclopedia. Sometime between last night and tonight I realized you're my missing link. Since coming to England, I've been my happiest right here in this cupboard, with you." Plonking herself on my lap, she straddles me.

Neither of us are sober, but this feels like Christmas already. I don't want any present other than the one currently sitting on top of me. "Perhaps we should deck this cupboard in boughs of Holly. One arm here, a leg there—"

"Kiss me, you muppet," she orders, taking my face between her hands and planting a smacker on my lips.

As we kiss, the lights go out — but I'm pretty sure the stationery storeroom is glowing bright as a neon. I'm pretty sure you could see how lit up I am even if you were the man on the Moon.

One of Holly's kisses and I'm already, *Och aye, she's fine.* So fine that one kiss and all I crave is Holly for now and for ever after...

EPILOGUE

Holly in Scotland

As we drive through the gates between towering pine trees laden with snow, I've never been so terrified in all my life. I'm more than a little in awe of Clyde and the prospect of meeting his family makes my stomach churn.

The castle tower looms above the tree canopy as we approach and it we could be driving onto the set of a film. As we exit the trees, I see part of the castle is in ruins, a tumble of stones. I feel like a part of me is crumbling too. I don't belong here. I don't belong with people who live in castles. I'm not sure I belong with Clyde if this is where he was born and brought up. Yes, I feel like an imposter because I am hopelessly out of, not only my depth, but my world.

As if reading my mind, Clyde puts his hand on my knee. "Don't fash, Holly. I'll take care of you," he grins.

"Fash?" I prickle, trying to swallow down my mounting fear. Is it too late to ask him to turn around and drop me off at the nearest train station?

"Don't fret. I know my family might seem...a bit much at first, but it's like anyone else's home."

Uh, no it's not. And I'm not just fretting. That doesn't come close. My fingers are digging holes in the car seat. Eyes glued to the castle, I'm freaking out. "Do you think this is such a good idea? I wasn't even invited," I whisper.

"You were invited. By me. Besides my parents are used to having extra house guests over the festive season," Clyde continues. "One more will make no difference. We have enough bedrooms."

And dungeons, no doubt.

The car crunches over the gravel of a courtyard and Clyde parks beside a pristine Land Rover. He puts his hand on mine. "Though, if you want to have an easy time of it, perhaps we'd best not say anything just yet about our being together. If they know we're more than friends, you'll no doubt get a grilling."

Mutely, I nod. I do not want a grilling. I imagine this is the sort of place where I could end up on a rotisserie spit grilled over an enormous fire.

Lights from the windows gleam weakly in the fading light of the day.

Feeling weak at the knees, I force myself to move and get out of the car. I peer upwards at the gigantic tower of the keep and feel like I have vertigo. Barking breaks the silence, the front door is thrown open and an assortment of dogs bound down the steps toward us. I brace myself, but thankfully, all they seem to want to do is lick me to death. Clyde crouches and takes a good licking for the team. The dogs clearly adore him.

"Get here!" barks a voice.

Startled, I jump.

The dogs immediately trot to the heels of the steely looking man standing because a coiffured, silver-haired lady at the top of the steps above us.

Clyde mounts the steps and shakes hands with the man before kissing the woman. If this is a Scottish family homecoming, it doesn't exactly augur a warm festive feeling.

Clyde introduces me to his parents, Marjorie and Hamish.

They're civil and too polite to show surprise, but their smiles never quite reach their eyes.

"Come on in, the pair of you, we've been waiting. It's been a while since Clyde brought any friends home," says his mother. "Clyde tells us you're from New Zealand, dear. It's lovely that you could join us. Aren't your own family missing you terribly?"

I may be being over-sensitive, but I feel like a charity case already and her words bite like she is digging her bony fingers into my arm. I mumble something in response and follow them inside, our footsteps echoing on the flagstone floors. Stag heads stare down from the walls in the hall. An enormous Christmas tree stands beside a grand sweeping staircase. Crossed swords gleam over a carved coat of arms above a crackling fire.

I'm shown to my room on the third floor of the main house. Stunned, I sit down on the enormous four-poster bed and listen to the wind moan outside. I'd quite like to bury my head beneath the bed covers and never come out again. What in heaven's name made me think this was a good idea? It's insane.

After a tepid bath, when I finally build up the nerve to go back downstairs and join everyone in the banqueting hall for their Christmas Eve drinks party, the first person I spot laughing with Clyde's mother is Clyde's lady friend, Olivia. Oh, joy. I think I'd rather be spending my Christmas Eve alone in my apartment in Burtonbridge. I already feel like the spare wheel. Olivia is in a shimmering midnight blue dress with a tartan sash across one shoulder. She looks very much at ease in her surroundings.

Clyde already appears to be in the thick of some sort of confrontation with his father, and I'm not sure I want to go there either. And, oh my Lord, he's wearing a kilt. The thighs on that man! Need to distract myself right now or I'll do something unseemly.

Thankfully, the waiter is very chatty…and has such a thick Scottish accent he's impossible to understand. I nod and do my best to look entertained. It's only after ten minutes of me asking about his work in the castle that I realize he's a cousin of Clyde's, not the waiter.

More guests arrive and the atmosphere in the Great Hall begins to thaw. Almost.

Most of the evening, I find myself chatting to random guests wishing Clyde and I didn't have to hide our relationship from anyone. This would be so much easier with him by my side. Even if I did succumb to temptation. Has he got anything on under his kilt? It's a very distracting thought. Whenever, Clyde does come over, I immediately feel nervously excited. I gabble. Before I know it, he's gone again, talking to another of the guests.

After one too many glasses of mulled wine, I begin to relax and would even go so far as to say I enjoy myself. I spend far too much of the evening imagining de-kilting my man.

Toward midnight, some of the guests begin to thin out, and I finally pluck up courage to gravitate toward the hearth where Clyde and his father appear to be growling at one another in low voices. It's difficult not to eavesdrop.

"It's a criminal waste of your talent and brains. I'm not changing my will unless you agree to finish your degree."

"Suit yourself," says Clyde.

"Damn it, lad. I can't understand why you have to make life so difficult for yourself. What were you thinking? That you'd seriously sacrifice everything for this stupid notion of yours? To become a poet. How is a poet going to be able to afford the upkeep on an estate like this for God's sake?"

"More to the point, how does poor Olivia feel about you not inheriting?" says his mother, stepping into the fray.

On the sidelines, I swallow. Beg pardon? *What's Olivia got to do with it?*

Clyde glances in Olivia's direction, then toward me. "I'm not *happy* about it, but you're not going to force me to change my mind about anything," he mutters.

"Force you? I'm not trying to do anything of the sort. You seem perfectly capable of fucking up your life without any help from the pair of us. Of all the stubborn idiotic..." — Hamish's voice rises in volume. The remaining guest are beginning to turn their heads, listening in — "You're a dreamer lad, and quite frankly a bloody embarrassment to the family name. I'm astounded Olivia hasn't dropped you like a hot coal!"

Hang on, what? WTF?

There's an ominous silence. A muscle works in Clyde's jaw and his fists are clenched at his sides. I've stopped breathing altogether. My head is reeling, trying to make sense of what I've just heard, waiting to hear what he says next.

Marjorie steps between them. Her smile looks strained. Her voice rasps. "Hamish. Clyde. Please, this is neither the time nor place. Poor Olivia."

Poor Olivia? Poor Olivia???

The night of the staff Christmas party, Clyde swore to me they were just friends. I'd asked him if there was anything between them at all, and he'd flatly denied it.

With what looks like a concerted effort, Hamish laughs and clamps his hand on Clyde's shoulder. "Perhaps you should speak to her, old chap."

Clyde shrugs him off. He goes to speak to Olivia, and I feel a little part of my heart crumble. I should not have got my hopes at. I knew this whole situation was insane. I don't feel sorry for Olivia at all as her eyes spark in my direction. She looks uncomfortable — she has high flashes of color in her cheeks and she's twisting her glass around and around in her hands — but she has no right to look uncomfortable! I'm the one who's out of place. Out of my depth. Why would Clyde hide their relationship from me? Why has he even brought me here. I put down my glass.

I think Olivia must have said something because Clyde spins around guiltily.

I will not give him the satisfaction of knowing how devastated I am, but there is zero point hanging around to be humiliated. Head held high, eyes welling, I make a beeline for the exit.

Clyde steps into my path.

"I'm going to bed," I say through gritted teeth. I seem to have developed a pain in my chest which is making breathing difficult.

"Please, Holly. Let me explain," he says.

"Now you want to explain? Now when I'm stuck in the middle of the god-forsaken bloody highlands miles from...from...bloody anywhere? Explain what exactly? I think everything's clear. I think everyone heard about you and poor bloody Olivia, you dick." I stamp my foot.

"Did she just call him a duck?" I hear someone say.

"Oh, shut up!" I yell, glaring at them. " I called him a dick. D.I.C.K!"

It's not my finest hour. I glance in Olivia's direction to find I'm not the only one with tears glittering in my eyes. Marjorie is at Olivia's side, a protective arm around her shoulders. I need to get out of here before I disgrace myself any further. Clenching my fist, I blink furiously against the dam of tears.

"You should never have brought me here. And you should've told me you were still involved with Olivia," I hiss at Clyde.

"I'm sorry. But look, it's not like that. It's old news. And complicated. And it's honestly nothing."

Nothing? "It doesn't look like nothing from where I'm standing! It's not nothing to me!" The lump in my throat is threatening to asphyxiate me.

"For God's sake, Holly, it's not what you think!" snaps Clyde.

I take a step backwards and stare at him in shock. It's not like him to lose his temper.

"I'm sorry," he says, holding his hand up as if in surrender. "I didn't mean for any of this..." He falters and looks helplessly over his shoulder toward Olivia.

That's it. "Look," I say waspishly, "I didn't mean to cramp your style. I've no idea why you invited me, and I don't want to know. But it would have been nice to know you and Olivia were...were...an item, before I accepted your invitation and hauled my backside all the way to bonnie bloody Scotland." My voice has grown cold and brittle.

"It's not like that. We're. Not. Dating," he says, annunciating his words carefully.

"What do you mean you're not dating?" His mother, Marjorie's voice cuts across the room.

Olivia puts her glass down and clasps her hands together. "The truth is...God this is so...um...awkward." She takes a breath. "Clyde and I broke up a while ago." Her voice trembles. "We just haven't had the opportunity to tell anyone. Until now." She grimaces.

"Though there have been plenty of opportunities," mutters Clyde under his breath.

"So you did go out with one another?" I ask, glowering.

With an effort, he nods miserably, his lips compressed into a tight line.

I sigh. I feel disappointed. I feel deceived. I feel maimed, as if I've thrown my heart into an animal snare and iron claws have snapped shut around it.

"Oh, for God's sake," snarls his father from across the room apparently not giving a damn that everyone is listening in on the conversation now. "I can't say I'm surprised. This is what comes from dropping out of Oxford. Can you honestly blame Olivia for dumping you? You have zero prospects. Trust you to mess up the one good thing you had going for you."

Wow, I think, what a pompous Scottish asshole.

"Wow," I say aloud and somewhat defensively. "That's harsh." Why am I coming to Clyde's defense when he's lied to me? Why am I putting myself in the firing line?

"I beg your pardon?" Hamish growls, his eyes bulging at me.

Oops, perhaps I spoke a little too loudly.

"Perhaps it's Clyde's pardon you should be begging," I say, conjuring up a smile from somewhere. "How do you even know this is his fault?" Perhaps it's the teacher in me coming out. Shouldn't every parent protect and nurture their own children?

Clyde puts a hand on my arm. "Don't bother."

"That is exactly your problem, son." His father stalks over and prods him so hard in the chest Clyde takes a step backward. "You don't bother. You can't be bothered. If anything is hard work, you take the easy way out and run a mile."

I put a hand on his father's chest and step between them. "That's not true, actually!" I say. "If you knew your son at all, you'd know Clyde is extremely hard-working. His team at Burtonbridge only have praise for him. High praise. And Clyde has every right to pursue his dreams. He's probably got more talent in his little finger than the rest of this family has in its entire history…"

The room falls silent again. Oh, hell. Why not insult the whole clan while I'm at it? In for a penny, in for a pound. "You should be proud of him. He's not only a grafter, he's gifted with words. He's a brilliant poet. I think any woman who ended up with him would be extremely lucky."

His father couldn't look more taken aback than if I'd slapped him. I'm fairly gobsmacked by my about turn myself.

His mother claps. "A woman like you?" she asks. Thank God someone is finding this entertaining.

Perhaps I should go and pack my bags now. I don't think I could've made the situation any less festive or more strained if I'd stripped and run around the room naked. I'm so not welcome here. There is an air of festive silence. A choir in my head starts singing, *Silent night, holy night…*

Clyde, my man of words, is ominously mute.

After all I've just said and done, he's staring at Olivia with an agonized expression on his face. Again.

Okay, I've practically thrown myself at his feet and declared my undying love which even his mother acknowledged, but not Clyde. I think I'm done here. Really, really.

Move your feet, Holly!

Like a tin soldier I march toward the door.

What are my chances of getting an Uber in the Scottish Highlands? Less than zero, I imagine. I trip over someone's foot and grab hold of the doorframe to support myself. "Shit! This is so shit!" I mutter.

"Wait! Excuse me, I have an announcement to make," I hear Olivia say behind me in a shrill voice. I'm not hanging around to hear this. "Holly, stop! Don't you dare leave! Not yet," she orders.

Against all reason and better judgement, I slowly turn around to face them all, my teeth gritted, a rigor mortis smile fixed on my face.

"Darlings, I just need to say something." She hangs her head and then raises her chin defiantly. "It's a little embarrassing…" She titters nervously and then clears her throat. "Clyde is one of my oldest and dearest friends. But…we should never have gone out with one another in the first place and that was entirely my fault." She grimaces. "And…ah…" She raises one hand while she takes a fortifying slug of her drink. "And whatever I feel for Clyde, *felt* for Clyde, it clearly isn't reciprocated. Because…because he'd rather be with someone else. That woman over there." She points at me with her glass and as everyone in the room turns to stare, I want to shrink into my shoes. "Which is terribly disappointing, but the truth."

I cannot breathe. I feel as if I've been buried beneath the cold stone slabs of the castle.

"But!" shouts Olivia above the hubbub. "I haven't finished!"

God preserve me.

"What I'm trying to say is, I guess I'll get over this. I'll get over Clyde. In fact, we all need to get over this." She draws a circle in the air with her glass, sloshing wine. "It wasn't Clyde who messed up our relationship…it was me." She raises her chin defiantly. "I was unfaithful, so I threw it all away." She suddenly glares in my direction. "Do not throw what you two have away."

I don't know about throwing it away, but I want to throw up because it looks like Olivia still isn't done with me yet.

"Also…also, I think it's time Clyde came clean," she says, looking wistfully at him. "Go on!"

My heart feels like it's been skewered by one of the swords on the wall. I'm not sure I can take much more of this.

"About what?" Clyde growls.

"About the fact you are totally and desperately in love with Holly Hadaway!"

Eyes turn again in my direction. My mouth falls open and I snap it shut.

"The Kiwi? But she's just a work colleague," says his father.

"Oh shut up, Hamish. Is this true?" demands his mother.

A tentative smile grows on Clyde's face. For the first time that evening, I see his eyes blaze. "One hundred per cent true," he says, taking both my hand in his. "I'm sorry I've been such an ass. I should've told you. I should have told everyone."

"Told us what?" I ask.

He presses his forehead against mine. "Everything," he whispers. "About the Liv situation. I didn't want to put her in an awkward position. She is a friend."

I lean back to get a better look at him. His forehead is creased with concern.

"And she's right when she said, I should have told you I am hopelessly and irretrievably in love with you," he announces.

"Oh," I say, as eloquent as ever.

"There's no way in hell you're running off without me," he says, gripping my hand tighter. "I think this calls for an elopement, don't you?"

"A what?"

"An old-style elopement. What do you say? Please elope with me?"

I'm too stunned to say anything. I open my mouth to speak, but he cradles my face between his hands and plants a fierce kiss on my lips in front of everyone.

There is a spatter of applause.

"Oh, for goodness sake!" booms his father's voice. "Not in public. Get a room! There's enough of them in this bloody castle."

"For once, my father is speaking sense," says Clyde, leading me out the door.

He pulls me, not toward the staircase as I'm expecting, but toward the door to the keep tower.

"Where are we going?" I ask in a small voice. Call me paranoid, but I'm still not totally convinced I'm not going to be punished.

He smiles back at me as he leads me up the stone stairwell, kilt swinging enticingly. "To the very top. To a wee room. One with a dodgy lock on the door."

A frisson of excitement flutters through me. The temperature of the tower drops the higher we go. At the very top of the keep is a small turret room most of it occupied by a huge wooden four-poster bed. On the floor beside it is a vase of roses, two crystal flute glasses and a bottle of champagne.

"You had this planned all along?" I say.

"*Och*, I wouldn't say it went exactly according to plan..." Clyde shuts the door firmly behind us and smiles roguishly. "But I cannae deny I had something like this in mind. I've been thinking about it most of the drive cup to Scotland in fact. I had to keep my distance this evening or I would have dragged you up here hours ago."

His words are heartwarming, but I can't help shivering even as he gathers me into his arms.

"Too cold?" he asks, kissing my nose which by now is probably as red as Rudolph's.

It's bloody freezing in here. I can't imagine what it's doing to his nether regions in that kilt. "Well, I'm not complaining, but I *can* see my breath," I say.

"At least we won't need to worry about warm champagne."

I giggle, my eyes alighting on the bed. It looks very inviting, heaped high with comforters and blankets.

"Is this your cunning ploy to get me under those covers?" I ask.

"However did you guess?" he growls, kissing me again.

His tongue sends tendrils of heat shooting to my core. I lean into him, hungry for more and feel the hard pack of his...sporran?

"That's some very hairy tassels you have there," I giggle. "What do you keep in it?"

He flicks back the layers of comforters and blankets with one hand and more or less throws me onto the bed. "If you're patient you might find out," he says, caging me between his arms, his deep Scottish burr sending a shiver of anticipation to my core.

"Let's stay here forever and throw away the key," I whisper.

"Aye, that's the general idea. Feeling any better yet?" asks Clyde, looking also almost cross eyed with lust.

My expression must mirror his. "It would be even better if we had less clothes on," I murmur, sliding my hand up his thigh beneath his kilt.

"Holly, hold on—"

I keep a hold on. I kiss him to shut him up. I kiss him to show him how much I want him. I kiss him because being with Clyde is the best place in the whole world to be. Under the covers, we impatiently undress one another.

It may be the chill in the air, but I cannot get close enough to Clyde. I want to be smothered. I want all of him.

Downstairs, the party may be continuing. Or maybe not. I couldn't care less. In this turret room, it goes from freezing to tropical in a hot second.

"When are you actually going to tell me how you feel about me?" he asks, pausing, hovering above me.

"Now?" I yelp, tugging at him feverishly. "You ask me this now?"

He grins wickedly, teasing and waiting with the patience of a saint.

I'm not feeling very saintlike. I'm hot with desire. "If you must know, I *feel* wicked. And sinful. I feel like the kid who already unwrapped her Christmas present on Christmas Eve."

He laughs. "And?"

"And talking of wrappings...do you have any?" I feel emboldened and impatient.

He laughs again and opens his sporran. He flaps a foil packet. "What, these?"

"Yes, condoms!"

While he sits back on his haunches, tearing open the condom packet he adds, "And was there something else you wanted to say?"

"Please? Please! What else is there to say?"

He quirks a brow. He wants more words, but his tender kisses, his tongue and the light touch of his teeth have already reduced me to a molten lava pool incapable of reasoned thought. All I know is I want him and...

"I love you!" I say. "Now will you please, please, please f—"

"It'd be my pleasure!" he says, beaming, "but first..." He disappears beneath the covers and his mouth begins to make sweet poetry of its own.

There are no adequate words. I writhe. I am slain. I am his entirely. In a very unladylike manner, I gasp and clutch fistfuls of his hair. "Holy...Sweet mother of...Merry Christmas!" I yell.

From somewhere deep beneath the covers comes a muffled response. "Merry Christmas, my Holly ever after."

Are you ready for another story by Anna Foxkirk? How about spending New Year's Eve in the land Down Under with *Alice in Wanderlust*?

ALSO BY ANNA FOXKIRK

More books to fall in love with in the Passport to Love series:

Alice in Wanderlust

The Worst Noelle

Be My Valerie

Holly Ever After

And coming in 2024...

Alice and the Impossible Game

Want to read a snippet of *Alice in Wanderlust*?

Chapter One

"Alice? You still here?" Roger hollers from somewhere in the bowels of the pub.

I pause, a bead of perspiration trickling down the side of my face. Hands immersed in hot soapy suds, I'm in the kitchen out the back of the Jolly Roger Inn scrubbing at pie crust that's superglued itself around the edge of a dish. I listen, puffing at my hair flopping into my eyes, uncomfortably aware of perspiration itching along my hairline and trickling down the sides of my face.

Roger is silent for now, so I resume my scrubbing.

Tilly, my twin sister, is proving about as easy to shift as this oven-baked grime. If only I could figure out how to persuade her it's time we moved on. Our year traveling together has ground to a halt. Catching glimpses of my reflection in the window above the sink isn't helping the head of steam I'm building up about our predicament. I want out of Sydney; Tilly seems to have become welded to the place.

I glance again at the clock on the wall. Everyone else has already left the building, except for Roger, the owner of this shithole, and me. I've only been working here for three weeks, but it's been long enough to figure out Roger is only *jolly* when the occasion suits him or when laughing at his own inappropriate jokes. It's amazing that any sane woman would find him remotely attractive, but only last week, Kylie, one of my co-workers confessed, with a snigger, that she'd let Roger have his jolly way with her in a cubicle of the Ladies'. The very idea makes me nauseous. To my mind, Roger's not so much a Jack Sparrow, as Kylie would have us imagine, as Jack Rodent, a scurrying scurvy bilge rat sniffing out his next victim.

If only I'd had the gumption to refuse to work the additional shift this week but lured by holiday rates and the need to pay rent on our apartment (because Tilly never seems to have a cent to her name), I've now worked five consecutive days since Christmas. Roger's take on my situation is that as the new kid on the block I'm not in a position to negotiate, but — Ho, bloody ho! — 'positions are always negotiable'.

I do not want to dwell on the greasy smirk on his face when he said those words, nor the fact he's becoming increasingly matey.

After drying the pans on the draining board, I throw everything back in the appropriate cupboards as fast as I can. Unfortunately, a pan lid clatters to the floor with all the discretion of clashing cymbals.

I freeze.

Whistling and footsteps head in my direction and the hairs on the back of my neck stand to attention as Roger swaggers in.

"Ahoy, my lovely! Still here? Anyone would think you were reluctant to leave me."

"Just finishing off," I say, hurriedly wiping down the worktops, my skin prickling as he leans against the doorframe and studies my every move. How is it, I wonder for the gazillionth time, that Tilly can land a glamorous job singing with a band and serving cocktails in a flashy nightclub, while I'm stuck sweating over dishes and fending off the scourge of Sydney? Oh yes, it probably has something to do with the fact that Tilly is screwing the nightclub owner, Axel.

"Fancy a nightcap, doll?" Roger winks.

I'm never exactly sure if he's calling me *doll* or *darl*, but either way I'd rather walk the plank. "Thanks, but I'm knackered. Not tonight." Not any night.

Drying my hands on my apron, I hang it up. As I shrug into my denim jacket and sling the shoulder strap of my handbag over my head, I'm aware of Roger stroking his beard. I know I'm nothing to write home about, especially not in my current swampy state, but the way he's eyeing me up you'd think I was drop dead gorgeous.

A thick hairy arm bars my exit from the premises.

"Right. See you tomorrow then," I say.

Roger doesn't budge.

Panic fluttering in my chest, I consider my options. Sadly, I have none of Tilly's acerbic wit or tongue-lashing confidence. Despite being her identical twin, she's the sort of siren who can sink a man with a heart-piercing glare or lure him into her arms (and bed) with a provocative whisper. We may be twins, but as far as my understanding of men goes, she was born fifteen minutes and about a hundred light-years ahead of me.

"Come on, Bucko! The night is but young," says Roger.

"I'm exhausted. Roger, excuse me. Please could you let me pass."

Slowly, miraculously, he moves enough to leave a tiny fissure through which I can squeeze, but as I rush towards it, his arm shoots out again. I skid to a halt, my heart skittering.

"I've been meaning to ask, when are you and me going on a proper date, Alice?"

I titter nervously. "Oh, I don't know. We're both busy people." *Maybe when Darling Harbor freezes over.*

"And busy people need to have fun. Look, I've done the roster for the next few days. I put you down to work during the day on New Year's Eve, but I've given you the evening off." He grins exposing yellowed teeth. "We could splice the mainsail together."

Excuse me? I want to gag. I have no interest in splicing anything with Roger. But how to talk my way out of here? "Well, thank you. That sounds like an interesting idea, but I—"

"Great. I'll hold you to that. I'm working on pulling in a few favors, pulling a few strings ..." He taps his bulbous red nose as if he has a great secret. "If all works out, maybe that won't be all I'm pulling. We'll bung some fire in the hole yet, eh?"

I don't know about fire, but I'd like to put a rocket under him and blast him into the stratosphere. The man is a monster. I glower at him. "We can discuss this some other time. I'm too tired to think straight right now…I'm. Going. Home," I say annunciating my last words very deliberately.

There is a rumble beneath our feet — perhaps an articulated truck passing by or a small earthquake — enough to rattle the plates and dishes on the shelves and for Roger to be momentarily distracted.

Taking full advantage, I dash beneath his arm quicker than a fox. As I rush through the gap, a hand connects with my backside and a low jeer of laughter follows me out of the restaurant onto the dark street.

Creep!

I break into a run and don't stop until I've rounded the corner of Dalgety Road. I gasp for breath. *I can't believe the disgusting rat slapped my backside!* I'm furious and ashamed. I should report him to someone … but who? And what would that achieve? I'd be out of a job, and even if I've no intention of staying any longer than I have to there are still bills to pay. What I need to do is persuade Tilly it's time to moving on. Sooner rather than later. Find work elsewhere. I can't stay working at the Jolly Roger – scrubbing dishes is the least of my worries.

Glancing over my shoulder, as I continue to jog up the street, I can't help worrying that he could be following me. Imagine if Roger knew where we lived. Where *I* lived. A shudder runs through me. Ugh. God forbid.

Tilly has more or less moved in with her clubbing boyfriend. I don't really blame her. It must be much nicer sharing silk sheets and a king-sized waterbed with Axel, than sharing the lumpy futon and cramped studio flat with me. Still, I can't help wishing she was around a bit more.

If wishes were horses, beggars would ride. Mum's voice in my head makes me smile and I finally slow down to a walk.

The last time I saw Tilly was Christmas morning. I made the mistake of bringing up the subject of our truncated gap year and travel plans, and a row exploded between us in spectacular festive fashion. It's nothing unusual for the two of us to bicker, but that had been about as close as we've come yet to going our separate ways – something I promised Mum would never happen. For all the stress and headaches my sister gives me, I would never leave her in the lurch. It's about time I called a truce. Or at least attempt to make contact with her.

I take out my cellphone and call her, but she doesn't answer. Maybe she's still pissed off with me. Maybe she's too busy having a life. Maybe it shouldn't always be me having to—

All holy crap! I leap out of my skin as something darts across my path and hisses — a bloody cat.

My heart pummels against my ribcage and I bend double trying to catch my breath. "Bloody scaredy cat!" I yell after it. Look who's talking.

A sob escapes me.

It takes a few deep breaths and a stern talking to myself and blowing my nose, before I get my nerves back under control. If anyone was watching me they'd think I'd lost the plot entirely.

I start walking again and my legs feel like jelly. I wanted this adventure, I remind myself. I wanted nothing more than to see the world and live…but some days I feel like I might as well be on my own. I never realized traveling with Tilly would mean spending so much time alone.

Want to find out what happens next to Alice? Grab your copy right here!

Coming in 2024: *Alice and the Impossible Game*

You can preorder here:

Amazon preorders

Other stores

AUTHOR'S NOTE

HAPPY HOLIDAYS and THANK YOU!

Dear reader,

I hope you loved reading Holly Ever After. If you did and would like to leave a short review that would be champion! It doesn't need to be long, but your feedback is invaluable to me as an author as it helps other readers find my fiction. I'd love your help spreading the word!

If you really really loved Holly, why not join my Facebook den of readers: Down to Earth https://www.facebook.com/AnnaFoxkirk/followers

Before you go, let me wish you all the very best for the festive season, as well as your very own Holly Ever After—even if you're stuck in a stationery closet somewhere!

Warm wishes,

Anna x

WANT TO STAY IN TOUCH?

If you'd like to be the first to hear news from me, be sure to sign up to my newsletter. Subscribers receive bonus content, early cover reveals, sneaky snippets of stories in the pipeline. I'd love to connect with you!

Sign up to my newsletter here:

Newsletter

If you're reading a paperback copy then please find my newsletter sign up details on my website: www.annafoxkirk.com

NEW BOOK ON ITS WAY…

For fans of close proximity, fake dates and holiday romances…

After 'Alice in Wanderlust', escape with this roadtrip romcom 'Alice and the Impossible Game'.

Printed in Great Britain
by Amazon